frankie murphy's

KISS LIST

frankie murphy 's

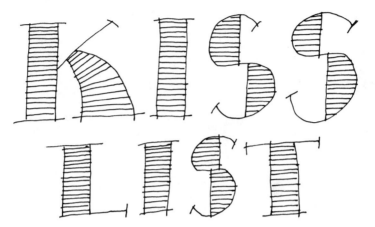

KISS
LIST

DONNA GUTHRIE

SIMON & SCHUSTER BOOKS FOR YOUNG READERS
Published by Simon & Schuster
New York   London   Toronto   Sydney   Tokyo   Singapore

SIMON & SCHUSTER BOOKS FOR YOUNG READERS
Simon & Schuster Building, Rockefeller Center
1230 Avenue of the Americas, New York, New York 10020
Copyright © 1993 by Donna Guthrie
All rights reserved including the right of reproduction
in whole or in part in any form.
SIMON & SCHUSTER BOOKS FOR YOUNG READERS
is a trademark of Simon & Schuster.
Designed by Vicki Kalajian.
Manufactured in the United States of America

10   9   8   7   6   5   4   3   2

Library of Congress Cataloging-in-Publication Data
Guthrie, Donna. Frankie Murphy's kiss list / by Donna W. Guthrie.
p.   cm. Summary: All the boys in the sixth grade get involved
when Frankie, the new kid, makes a bet that he can kiss
every girl in their class before the last day of school.
[1. Wagers—Fiction. 2. Schools—Fiction.] I. Title.
PZ7.G9834Fr   1993   [Fic]—dc20   93–16172   CIP
ISBN: 0–671–75624–9

To Erin and Mollie Ricker,
with special thanks to
Piper Beatty and Piper Foster

one

"Some girls' lips are real fat and puffy," said Frankie Murphy. "And when you kiss them, it feels like you're kissing marshmallows." Frankie lowered his voice to a whisper. "While other girls—other girls—they hold their lips real tight making their mouths all hard and tight like the seam on a baseball."

Travis Marshall stepped away from the group of sixth-grade boys. They were acting as if they'd just heard the punch line to a dirty joke. Travis looked up at the blue April sky and waited for the morning bell. Like always, Frankie Murphy was the center of attention.

"When girls hold their lips tight like this," said Frankie as he puckered his mouth, "it feels about as good as kissing the backboard on a basketball court."

Travis shoved his fists into the pockets of his Oakland A's jacket and looked around. It seemed that ever since Frankie Murphy had arrived at King Elementary, people treated him like he was the resident expert on everything. And Travis was tired of it.

"I guess in my lifetime, I've kissed about five, maybe six hundred girls."

Frankie shouted over to Travis.

"Are you getting all this, Marshall? Nerds like you can use all the help they can get."

Travis shook his head. "No," he said. "I think what you're saying is a lot of bull."

The other boys stared at him.

"The way I see it," said Travis, "you're only twelve years old. Even if you started kissing girls in first grade, you'd have to have kissed a hundred girls a year for the past six years to kiss six hundred. Nobody can do that."

"Sure he could," said Marcus Turnby. Marcus was the school genius, and math was his favorite subject. "Mathematically speaking, it's possible."

Marcus took out his pocket calculator and punched in the numbers. His dirty blond hair stood up in short spikes around his head making him look as if he'd touched a live outlet. "That's only 8.3 girls a month or .27 girls a day."

"But that's my point," said Travis. "How would anybody kiss .27 girls?" He stepped forward so that he stood eye to chin with Frankie. "It can't be done."

Frankie smiled down at those around him. Frankie was a good six inches taller than any of the other boys. "I didn't say I kissed all those girls while I was in school, did I?"

"No, you didn't say that," said Marcus. "To be precise, you said that you kissed five or six hundred girls in your lifetime."

"You forget," said Frankie, "that while you guys were growing up here in this hick town, I was living in Philly. I've been spending every summer since I was six years old at the Jersey Shore." Frankie let out a long low whistle. "Now, Jersey girls, they really know how to kiss."

"Right," said Tony Foley, Frankie's best friend. "You told me about those girls from New Jersey." The boys crowded closer to Frankie to hear more.

It's always like this, thought Travis. Ever since

Frankie Murphy arrived in Harpersville, he's been telling everybody how much better things were in Philadelphia. At first, Travis had tried to be friends with Frankie. He'd invited him over to his house after school, introduced him to some of the guys, even taken him down to the Y to play basketball. But everything Travis showed him, Frankie would compare to something bigger and better in Philadelphia.

"This place doesn't have a sports team or a mall or even a video arcade," said Frankie. "Heck, this town doesn't even have its own exit off the turnpike. How bad is that?"

"You'll like it once you get used to it," Travis had told Frankie. "The people are really nice, and besides Indianapolis isn't that far away. You can go there on weekends and do stuff."

"What stuff?"

"Like the zoo, the Hoosier Dome, the Children's Museum. Last spring our Boy Scout troop went to Market Square Arena to hear a concert."

"Concert?" Frankie laughed. "Oh, right, Marshall, that's just what I'd want to see. A bunch of guys dressed up like penguins playing violins."

"It wasn't just violins, it was the whole orchestra," said Travis. "You just have to give this place a chance. It's a great town."

"Sure," said Frankie, "so is Mister Rogers' neighborhood, but who wants to live there? I think this place is full of ugly girls and nerdy Boy Scouts. I hate it here."

After that Travis didn't try to defend Harpersville anymore. In fact, he tried not to spend that much time with Frankie. But others did. The boys in the class looked up to Frankie as the expert on everything.

The morning bell rang throughout the school yard. Travis stood on tiptoe and looked Frankie right in the eye. "If you're such a big shot, prove it."

"Prove what?" said Frankie.

"Prove that you've kissed a hundred girls."

Frankie laughed. "How? Call all the girls I've kissed and have them write you a letter?" He pointed at Travis. "He acts just like his father, the lawyer. He wants the letters notarized and sanitized, so they're legal."

Tony Foley nudged the boy next to him. "Can you believe this guy talking to Frankie like that? What a jerk!"

The other boys laughed.

Typical, thought Travis. As far as they were concerned Frankie was the coolest kid that had ever come to Harpersville. He had everything. He was a great basketball player, a cool dresser, and practically every girl in the whole school had a crush on him because he looked like Jason Priestley.

The second bell rang and the crowd moved toward the door. Travis grabbed Frankie's arm. "Come on, Murphy, you're always telling us how great you are. Why don't you prove it? If you really kissed a hundred girls a year for the past six years, you could do it again."

Frankie brushed Travis's hand away and smoothed his leather jacket.

"There's only seven girls in our class, right?" Travis said.

"Six really," said Tony. "I don't think you should count Penelope Finchester. She's so weird, her own mother wouldn't kiss her."

"And we have five more weeks before we graduate. Right?" said Travis.

"Promoted," said Marcus. "To be exact, you don't graduate to junior high school, you get promoted."

Travis motioned for Marcus to be quiet. "Make a list," he said. "Make a list of all the girls in the class and kiss each one of them before the end of the year. If you're really as good as you say you are, you should be able to do that."

"He's right," said Marcus. He pulled the calculator from his shirt pocket. "The mathematical possibilities of a kiss list are very exciting." He punched the numbers quickly. "By my calculations that's exactly 1.4 girls a week for five weeks. That shouldn't be too hard." He grinned at the other boys. "And to make it more exciting, the two of you should make a wager," said Marcus.

"A wager? What's he talking about?" asked Frankie.

"You know," said Tony, "a bet. People do it all the time."

"Great idea," murmured Johnny Watson.

Travis stared Frankie in the eye. "I bet you can't do it. I bet you can't kiss all the girls in the sixth grade before the last day of school."

Frankie took off his Phillies cap and slipped it into his pocket. His hair was perfectly combed, Travis saw, no hat hair for Frankie. "Seven girls in five weeks?" He looked down at the tips of his Reeboks for a moment. "Shucks, that's easy. I could do it with my eyes closed."

Tony turned to the other guys, "And that's just the way he'll do it—with his eyes closed."

Travis held out his hand. "Do we have a bet then? Or are you chicken?"

"Of course I'm not chicken," said Frankie. "But what's in it for me?"

The late bell rang.

"I mean, here you are asking me to kiss all the girls in the sixth grade, even the ugly ones, right?"

Travis nodded.

"And what will you give me if I do it?"

Travis hesitated. "Five dollars?"

Frankie shook his head.

"Ten dollars?"

"Nope," said Frankie, "money's too easy. Your old man can give it to you." He studied Travis for a moment and then his eyes grew narrow and cold. "If I kiss all the girls in the sixth grade, I want you to give me something you really care about."

Travis looked around. Everybody was watching him. If he backed down now, he'd look like a jerk.

Frankie reached out and felt the embroidered *A* on the front of Travis's gold Oakland A's jacket. "If I kiss all the girls in our class, I want this," he said.

"The *A*?"

"No, stupid, the jacket."

"But I thought you were a Phillies fan."

"Of course, I'm a Phillies fan," said Frankie, "but gold's my favorite color. So, when I win I want this jacket. What do you say?"

Travis shoved his sweaty palms deep into the pockets of the jacket and felt the soft cotton lining. He loved this jacket more than anything he owned.

His father had bought it for him on a business trip to California. He'd driven all the way to the stadium to buy it.

"What do you say, Marshall? Do you want to bet your jacket?"

"I don't know," said Travis. "This jacket means a lot to me. Nobody in the whole school has a jacket like this one."

"Right," said Frankie, "that's why I want it." He turned toward the others. "The way I look at it, I'm doing all the work. I mean, I have to kiss all those bimbos. Right?"

Bimbo was one of those Philly words that Frankie always used. It meant girl. Travis hated it.

"And if he's so sure I can't do it, he should be willing to put his jacket where his mouth is. Right?"

Tony and the others nodded.

Travis was about to object, but then he remembered something. He had an ace in the hole, his best friend, Annie Davis. She hated Frankie Murphy. She wouldn't kiss him in a million years. There was no way Frankie was going to win his jacket.

Travis held out his hand. "Okay," he said, "if you win, you get my Oakland A's jacket."

"One more thing," said Frankie, "no telling the girls."

"What?"

"I said, no telling the girls."

"Why?"

"Because I do my work in secret, so don't tell your buddy Davis about any of this." He turned to the group. "And the same goes for the rest of you. This is going to be just between us guys."

As the two boys shook hands, Marcus announced the conditions once more. "By the last day of school Frankie is going to kiss all the girls in the sixth-grade class."

"Including Penelope Finchester," added Travis. "He has to kiss her too."

Frankie shrugged. "It doesn't matter to me. I'll start with Finchester, if you want me to. Make the list. Who's keeping score?"

"I will," said Marcus. He took a small pad from his coat pocket. "When will you begin?"

"No time like the present," said Frankie. "Enjoy that jacket, Marshall," he added. "You won't have it much longer."

two

Through the open door of the gym, Travis watched Annie Davis run down the court shouting plays at the other girls. As she ran past, her long brown ponytail flicked back and forth. She nodded her head and signaled that she knew he was waiting for her. The two of them always walked home together. He and Annie had been best friends since kindergarten and lived only a few houses away from each other on the same street. If he finished band practice early, he'd wait for her. If she finished with basketball, she'd come to the band room and find him.

Up the court, Annie raced toward him. She was

11

smiling, showing her newly straightened teeth. The braces had come off only last week and she looked great. As she ran she dribbled the ball effortlessly in an easy rhythm. When she neared the hoop, she passed off to another girl and cheered when the ball went in. Annie was captain of the team and the best player in the whole school. Basketball meant everything to her. In fact, it was hard for Travis to think about Annie without a basketball in her hands.

From across the floor came the sound of Mrs. Klein's whistle, signaling practice was over. "Good work, girls, see you here tomorrow."

Annie waved at Travis. "I'll be there in a minute," she called. "Just let me get my jacket."

The other girls gathered up the balls and handed them to Penelope Finchester, the team manager. As each ball was dropped into the equipment bag, Penelope counted out loud, "One, two, three, four."

Penelope blew her nose in a wad of tissue and dabbed at her red, watery eyes. She was allergic to dogs, cats, trees, dust, and some people. Penelope's blond hair was pulled straight back into a rubber band making her pale face look even more homely. She wore baggy shorts and an oversized T-shirt that said SAVE THE GILA MONSTERS.

Typical, thought Travis, Penelope is always wanting to save something. Last year, in fifth grade, Penelope got a button maker for Christmas. She told everyone that her mother had seen it on the shop-at-home network at two o'clock in the morning and ordered it on the spot. No one seemed to think it was unusual for Penelope's mother to be up at two o'clock in the morning watching people sell button makers. Everyone knew the Finchesters were weird.

Now, every lunch period, you could find Penelope in the art room making buttons to sell. According to Penelope there were sixty-three animals on the endangered species list. She had a goal to make a button for every one of them.

So far she'd made buttons for the bald eagle, the gray whale, the spotted owl, and the California gnat catcher. In between animal buttons, she made buttons for special occasions. During National Library Week she'd made buttons with a red slash over a giant taco which said READ DON'T FEED.

No one ever bought any of Penelope's buttons. Most of the time she ended up giving her buttons away and begging people to wear them. As far as the kids were concerned, it was one more thing that made Penelope Finchester weird.

Penelope frowned. "There's one ball missing,"

she said to no one in particular. The other girls were putting on their jackets and gathering their books. They stopped what they were doing to look around.

From behind the bleachers stepped Frankie Murphy. "Looking for this?" he asked. He crossed the gym floor and dropped the missing ball into Penelope's bag.

Penelope's face turned a deep red and she lowered her eyes.

"Get a move on, Penelope," yelled Mrs. Klein. "Bring those balls in and put them away. We don't want to be here all night."

Travis watched in amazement as Frankie hoisted the heavy bag onto his shoulder. "I'll take it for you, just tell me where it goes."

Penelope blinked her watery eyes and pointed to Mrs. Klein's office.

Annie tapped Travis on the shoulder. "Okay, I'm ready. Let's go." She twirled the ball on her finger for a second, then dropped it and caught it neatly under her arm. "Unless you want to wait for Penelope."

"What are you talking about?"

"You haven't taken your eyes off her ever since you got here. Do you like her or something?"

"Get out of here," said Travis. He gave her a

friendly shove. "Penelope Finchester? She's weird!"

"Oh, she's not so bad, once you get to know her," said Annie. "She's just shy around boys. Around us girls, she's great." Annie handed Travis her book bag and the basketball, while she put on her jacket.

Travis took a deep breath. Annie smelled nice, a mixture of bubble gum, basketballs, and lemon soap.

As they walked out of the gym and down the hall, Annie bounced the ball beside her. "What was Mr. Wonderful doing in the gym today?"

"Who knows? Maybe's he's trying to pick up some new plays from you and the rest of the girls." Travis held the door open while Annie dribbled through to the outside.

"I doubt that," said Annie. "According to Frankie, he's the answer to the NBA."

The basketball stopped bouncing. Travis looked up.

Frankie Murphy and Penelope Finchester were walking out of the gym. Frankie was carrying Penelope's book bag and listening to something she was saying.

"I didn't know Frankie and Penelope were friends," said Annie.

"They aren't," said Travis. "He can't stand her."

Penelope continued talking, flapping her arms to

illustrate a point and giving a couple of shrill bird calls. Frankie leaned forward.

"You can't tell that by the way he's acting," said Annie. "They look like they're going together."

Frankie guided Penelope across the school yard. He slipped his arm around Penelope's shoulders as they walked toward First Avenue.

Annie turned to Travis. "Okay, what's going on? What's Mr. Stuck-on-Himself doing with Penelope?"

"How should I know?"

Annie brushed a loose strand of hair from her face. "Hey, you, this is Annie, remember me? We don't keep secrets from each other. We're friends."

Travis watched Frankie and Penelope walk down the street and out of sight. Maybe I should tell her, he thought. Maybe I should tell her about the bet.

Annie threw the ball up in the air and caught it on an open palm. "You don't have to tell me, but I know there's something going on."

"What are you talking about? Just because a guy and a girl walk home together doesn't mean they're going together," said Travis. "We walk home together every day and it doesn't mean a thing."

"Right," said Annie, "not a thing."

They crossed the avenue and headed toward their street. When they got to her front yard Annie said, "Do you want to come over later and shoot a few baskets?"

"I can't. We have band tryouts tomorrow for the spring concert. If I want to move up a chair, I have to practice." Annie walked through her front gate and let it click shut between them.

"You'll make it, you're the best clarinet player they have," she said. She turned to go inside.

"Annie," said Travis. "Do you like Frankie Murphy?"

"Who wants to know?" She threw the basketball over the gate and he caught it. "You asking for yourself or somebody else?"

"I want to know."

She smiled. "I think that Frankie Murphy is the biggest dork that has ever come to Harpersville. He walks around like he's got the keys to the ice-cream truck, and I can't stand him."

Travis laughed. It was just what he wanted to hear. He threw the ball back at her.

"And if you ever acted stupid like Frankie Murphy, I'd never talk to you again!"

"Really?"

She backed away, still smiling. "Don't look so serious. Frankie is in a class all by himself when it comes to being a jerk. You're nothing like him."

"Right," said Travis. "I'm nothing like him."

three

"I don't get it, Travis," said Mollie Sherman. "What does Penelope Finchester have the rest of us don't?" Band practice was over and only a few people had stayed late to rehearse some more for the spring concert.

Travis shrugged and took the mouthpiece off his clarinet. He had to hurry. Annie would be outside waiting for him.

"Well, whatever Penelope has, there's a lot of it," said Allison Caldwell. "She and Frankie Murphy have been acting like Ken and Barbie for the past week and a half. He walks her home every day, eats lunch with her. I even saw him in the art room helping with those stupid buttons of hers."

Mollie checked her reflection in the small mirror in her trumpet case. She clicked the case shut. "There are so many pretty girls in the sixth grade," said Mollie. "I just don't understand what Frankie sees in somebody like Penelope Finchester."

Marcus stuffed his sheet music into his brief-case. "Perhaps there's more to Penelope than first meets the eye." He winked at Travis. "In fact, I'd say there's a list of things that makes Penelope attractive."

Allison folded up her music stand and put it in her book bag. "Well, I don't get it. I didn't know Frankie even knew Penelope. Now, they're practically joined at the hip. If you ask me, the whole thing is very, very strange."

Mollie giggled. "Or maybe Frankie's working on his Eagle Scout badge and he has to be nice to weirdos."

"Don't be stupid," said Travis. "There's no badge like that." Travis was working toward being an Eagle Scout. "Besides, all the girls on the basketball team like Penelope. Annie says she's real nice once you get to know her."

Mollie made a face. "Oh, Annie and her team

think anybody's nice who can bounce a basketball." She picked up her trumpet case and her book bag. "Are you coming, Allison? I've got to get home, my mother is taking me shopping today for a new dress."

She turned to Marcus and Travis. "The invitations for my party go out on Saturday. You have one week to reply and if you don't, I'm inviting somebody else."

"Who cares?" said Marcus. "I don't like birthday parties anyway. People sitting around wearing stupid hats and watching somebody open all the gifts. It's dumb."

"That's all you know, Marcus," said Mollie. She threw her pink Esprit sweatshirt over her shoulders. "People haven't been wearing party hats since the second grade." She tied the sleeves of the sweatshirt into a big knot. "And for your information, 'Mr. I-Don't-Like-to-Go-to-Parties,' this is a very special birthday for me. I'll be thirteen and this party will also be my bat mitzvah."

Allison put her arm around Mollie. "A bat mitzvah is a very important event in the life of a Jewish girl. When you turn thirteen and you're Jewish, there's a special service at the synagogue. Mollie has to read this big part from the Torah. She's been taking Hebrew lessons for over a year to get ready."

Mollie nodded. "And afterward, my parents have invited all my friends and relatives over to the house for lunch. My mother is having the whole thing catered with all my favorite foods."

"I can hardly wait," said Marcus, "What are you having . . . corn dogs and pizza?"

"No, silly, this party will be really fancy, with tiny sandwiches and fruit punch. I asked my mother if everything could be pink and yellow because those are my favorite colors."

Marcus looked at Travis and rolled his eyes.

"And everybody who comes has to bring a present," said Mollie. "That's the way it's done."

"I knew there'd be a catch," said Marcus.

Allison sighed. "I wish I were Jewish, so I could have a bat mitzvah too."

"It figures," said Marcus. "You always want to do everything she does. I bet if Mollie drank cyanide, you'd probably want a sip. Why don't you ever think for yourself, Allison?"

"I do," said Allison, "and the thought that I have now is that you're a jerk." She picked up her blue Esprit sweatshirt, exactly like Mollie's, and put it around her shoulders. She checked Mollie's knot and tied her sleeves the same way.

Mollie took out a mirror from her purse, looked in it, and grimaced at her braces. "Did I tell you," said Mollie, "I asked my parents to hire a real band for the party?" She dropped the mirror into her purse and smiled. "So, if you want to come you better be nice to me."

"Nice to you?" said Marcus. "Not on your life. As I said before, I hate parties."

Mollie turned to Travis. "And if you come," she said, "you can't wear that!" She pointed to Travis's Oakland A's jacket slung over a chair. "You have to put on a suit and a tie and look decent."

Travis picked up his jacket and rubbed at a spot. He couldn't remember whether it was mud or chocolate pudding. "What do you mean?" he said. "This is decent. This is the most decent thing I own."

Travis looked at the spot. "Well, maybe I could have it cleaned. When's the party?"

"Travis," said Allison, "you may not understand, but this birthday party is very special for Mollie and she wants it perfect. You can't come looking like the bat boy for some stupid baseball team."

"A girl's bat mitzvah is almost as important as her wedding," said Mollie. "You wouldn't go to a wedding in that thing would you?"

"Maybe I would," said Travis. "But right now most of my friends are single."

"That's a good one." Marcus snorted. "Most of his friends are single."

Mollie looked disgusted. "Come on, Allison," she said, "let's go."

Allison tossed her flute into her book bag and picked up the empty case. "Are you two coming to the sixth-grade skating party tonight?"

"Absolutely," said Marcus. "Travis and I wouldn't miss it."

Mollie walked backward toward the door, pulling Allison after her. "Then save me a skate, Travis." She laughed. "Unless, of course, you and Annie are planning to skate together all night like you always do." Her shiny silver smile seemed to last long after she was out of the room.

"Girls!" said Marcus. "Who needs them?" He picked up his tuba and carried it to the front of the room and placed it on the wooden stand. "Well, are you ready to hear what happened today?"

Ever since the morning of the bet, Marcus had kept a detailed progress report on Frankie Murphy's kiss list.

Marcus glanced around the room to make sure they were alone. "Frankie decided tonight's the night," he whispered.

"The night for what?"

"Don't play stupid with me. You know. At the class roller skating party. Tonight, Frankie is going to kiss Penelope Finchester."

Travis closed his clarinet case and locked it with two sharp clicks. These daily reports on Frankie were getting on his nerves.

"I saw Frankie at lunch," continued Marcus. "He told me that he has it all planned."

"What do you mean?"

"Frankie wants you there, tonight."

"Why?"

"Because that way there's no mistake, he'll have proof. You and Annie are supposed to skate behind him during the first couples-only skate and watch him do it."

"He's going to kiss her with people watching? You got to be kidding!"

"Sure, he wants to make sure that everybody sees it. Frankie says that Finchester is the hardest, and after her, the list gets easy." Marcus paused. "Can you imagine what it would be like to kiss Penelope Finchester? Just the idea of it gives me the creeps."

Travis shivered. "It makes my stomach turn."

Marcus pulled two pieces of computer paper out of his pocket and handed one to Travis. "This is a list of all the girls in the sixth-grade class. The way I figure there's only four more weeks of school and he's got six girls to go."

"That's if he can kiss Penelope tonight, right?"

"Precisely," said Marcus. "The rules are that he has to have at least one witness. Tonight, he'll have the whole class watching."

Travis studied his list for a moment. "But how does Frankie even know she's going to be there tonight? She's never come to any of the class parties before."

"Are you kidding? Everybody knows she's hanging around with the best-looking boy in school. She wouldn't miss tonight for anything." Marcus checked his list against the numbers on his calculator. "The way I figure it, if it takes a week and a half for each girl, he's never going to make it. He's wasted too much time setting up Finchester."

Travis put on his jacket. The soft, smooth nylon was almost like silk. Spots or no spots, I really love this jacket, he thought.

"Hey, look at this." Marcus pointed to the list. "Katy O'Donnel and Ricky Romer both go to Frankie's church. Maybe he could kiss them during communion or something. That could cut two off his list right there."

"No way," said Travis. "People don't kiss in church."

"Sure they do," said Marcus. "I'm Episcopalian and we do it all the time. Right before the offering, the minister tells you to greet your neighbor. Everybody shakes hands or kisses the person next to them on the cheek. It's called the kiss of peace."

"But that's not really kissing," said Travis. "Kissing is lip to lip. Everybody knows that."

"Maybe so," said Marcus. "But you didn't say where and how people kiss when you made the bet." He licked the point of his pencil and made two small question marks by Katy's and Ricky's names. "I'd better check this out with Frankie and Tony and get the rules straight."

"But you're the judge. You're keeping score. You can say how it has to be done," said Travis. This was getting serious. If kissing in church counts, Frankie might win after all. All he'd have to do is some Sunday get Annie to go into some Episcopal church before the offering and when the minister says "Greet your neighbor," he'd turn and lay a kiss of peace right there in front of the whole congregation. It wasn't fair.

Marcus tucked the paper into his shirt pocket.

"Sometimes I think you're on his side," said

Travis. "Frankie has this whole thing planned out. And you're helping him."

"No I'm not," said Marcus. "It's just that I have to give the guy credit for the way he goes about things." Marcus folded his arms across his chest. "Look, Travis, the guy isn't stupid. He wants your jacket."

Travis felt the warmth of the jacket on his shoulders. "But when we made that bet, it was just for fun. We were just kidding around," said Travis. "He doesn't have to take it so seriously. It's only a bet."

"Only a bet!" said Marcus. "You challenged him in front of every boy in the sixth grade. He's got to do it now, it's a matter of pride."

Travis picked up his backpack and swung it over his shoulder. "I just didn't expect he'd go at it like this, that's all."

Marcus closed his briefcase and fiddled with the lock. He changed the combination every day.

"Who are the last four girls?" Travis asked.

"From memory? There's Terry Hays, Allison, Mollie, and your buddy, Annie."

Travis picked up his clarinet case. "Well, I don't know about the others but Annie isn't going to let the guy even near her."

Marcus looked at him. "You didn't tell her, did

you? This whole thing is supposed to be a secret just between us guys."

"No, I wouldn't do that," said Travis. "All I'm saying is that I know Annie and she can't stand the guy."

"That's what they all say. Wait till he turns on the charm. You've seen how he put the moves on Finchester? He has her smiling and laughing all the time. The guy really knows how to handle women."

"Well, he won't handle Annie," said Travis. "I know her."

Travis switched off the light in the band room. "Besides, the way I look at it, he has his work cut out for him just kissing Penelope."

"True," said Marcus. "All we've seen so far is him making buttons and walking her home."

"Right," said Travis, trying to make himself feel better. "There's a lot of difference between walking a girl home and kissing her."

Annie poked her head inside the room. "I'll say. You walk me home every night and you've never kissed me."

The two boys looked at each other. How long had she been standing there? What had she heard?

"Are you ready?" said Annie. "I have to get

home and get dressed for the skating party."

"Me too," said Marcus. He pushed past her through the door. "Don't forget, Travis, the first couples-skate . . . you have to be there!"

Annie gave Travis a strange look. "Are you and Marcus some sort of couple tonight?"

"Don't be stupid."

Annie stared at him for a couple of seconds, "Don't worry, Travis, I'm a lot of things, but I'm not stupid."

four

The spinning mirrored globe above Travis's head cast round shadows on the shiny floor of the roller rink and small gold circles on his Oakland *A's* jacket. He touched the list in his pocket again. He had gone over the names so many times he had the list memorized.

All around him kids were putting on skates while others stood by the railing, waiting for the party to begin. The Flying Wheels Roller Rink was packed with boys and girls from all over Harpersville. But Frankie Murphy and Penelope Finchester were nowhere to be seen.

Over the loudspeaker came the voice of the disc

jockey, "Welcome to the Flying Wheels Roller Rink, everyone. Tonight we'd like to give a special welcome to the sixth graders of King Elementary School.

"We hope all of you will enjoy your skating party tonight, and to get you off on the right foot, I'm going to play one of your favorites." The lyrics of "Born in the USA" filtered over the loudspeaker and skaters hurried toward the floor.

From the other side of the rink came Marcus, skating out of control, straight toward Travis. "Stop me!" yelled Marcus. "Somebody, stop me!" Travis held out his hand, but Marcus was going too fast to stop. He crashed into Travis with full force. They fell to the floor with a thud, landing in a twisted heap of arms, hands, and roller skates.

Marcus sat up and collected his calculator and pens which lay scattered on the floor. "This roller skating is totally overrated. I feel like a real klutz on these things."

"You are a real klutz," said Travis. He got up and brushed himself off.

"Don't just stand there," yelled Marcus, "give me a hand up!" Travis reached down and pulled him to his feet.

Marcus teetered a bit before getting his balance.

He straightened his tie. "Usually, I don't come to the skating parties," said Marcus. "I think they're boring." He tried to steady himself by leaning against the wall.

Marcus looked around. "Where's Annie?"

"I don't know. She called to tell me her parents couldn't find a baby-sitter so she's coming later with Reed."

Marcus lowered his voice. "How much do you think she heard today?"

"I'm not sure, I think—"

Mollie skated up to them. She twirled around once to show off her short yellow skirt and matching sweater. "Are you two going to stand here all night talking or are you going to roller-skate? This is a party, you know."

"We're having a private conversation here, Mollie," said Marcus. "This is guy stuff, no females allowed."

Mollie leaned against the railing and snapped her fingers. "I love this song, don't you?" The lights spun around as skaters flew past.

"Did I tell you I know how to skate backward?" said Mollie. "I come here on Saturdays for private lessons. My teacher says I have real talent."

"Talent?" Marcus laughed. "Since when is propelling yourself backward on eight little ball bearing wheels a talent?"

"My teacher says it takes skill and concentration to skate backward."

"Oh sure. You never know when a talent like that could come in handy. When could you use it? Parades? The Miss America contest? Or maybe a Roller Derby?"

"At least I can get across the floor without crashing into everybody, Marcus. Maybe you could use a few lessons yourself." She turned to Travis. "Do you want to skate with me, Travis?"

"Not right now, maybe later. I'm waiting for someone."

"Okay, but save a set for me." She skated backward toward the center of the floor, right into Frankie Murphy.

"Watch where you're going, you almost made me fall!" yelled Frankie. He had on a pair of gray Rollerblades, the same kind the high school kids wore. Travis looked down at his mud-brown rentals.

Mollie skated around Frankie backward, toward Travis.

"Where's Penelope? I thought you two were going together."

"Who told you we were going together?" asked Frankie. He eyed Travis suspiciously. "Are you spreading rumors about me again, Marshall?"

"Cool it, Frankie," said Travis. "I haven't said anything to anybody."

"Good." Frankie turned and surveyed the roller rink. "This place is a dump," he announced. "Back in Philly we have roller rinks twice this size. My cousin and I used to go skating all the time in this place where they had a restaurant, a bowling alley, and a video arcade all under one roof."

He pointed at the mirrored globe above his head. "Look at that old-fashioned thing up there. In Philly we had strobe lights connected to the music. Now that was cool."

"For your information these lights are very valuable, they're . . . they're . . ." Travis searched for the word.

"Antiques?" asked Frankie. "I know. It goes along with everything else in this hick town." He counted the list on his fingers. "Those little green benches on Main Street are antiques, the flower pots around the parking meters, and the fact that nobody ever locks their doors around here. This place looks like the movie set for *Lassie*."

Mollie giggled.

Frankie shook his head. "I don't know why my dad had to get transferred to this two-bit burg in the first place. I hate it here."

Travis glided forward, his fists clenched. "Nobody says you have to stay, Murphy. The street goes two ways." Frankie skated easily around him. "Hey, look at the lawyer's kid. He's a little grouchy, wouldn't you say?"

"He's right, Travis," said Mollie. "What's wrong with you?"

Frankie smiled at Travis. "Maybe he's just a little nervous about tonight?"

Tony Foley skated up and draped his arm across Marcus's shoulder. "Penelope had to help Mrs. Klein set up the gym for tomorrow's game," said Tony. "She'll be here soon and then we can get this whole thing started."

"Get what started?" asked Mollie. "What's going on?"

Frankie smiled at her. "Nothing for you to worry your pretty little head about."

Mollie beamed.

"This is just a something we have going between us guys to make life more interesting around here." Frankie held out his hand. "Do you want to skate?"

Before Mollie could answer, Allison glided up

and grabbed her arm. "Come over to the snack bar with me, right now," she said. "There's a boy I want you to meet."

Mollie batted her eyes at Frankie. "I'll be right back. Wait for me, will you?" The two girls skated away.

Frankie turned to Travis. "Well, Marshall, I see you're wearing my jacket."

"It's not yours yet," said Travis. "In fact, the way I see it, you've been all talk and no action."

Tony laughed and nudged Marcus. "Like I told your buddy Marcus, here, once Frankie knocks off Finchester, the rest will be a piece of cake."

Frankie motioned toward Mollie and Allison. "Did you see how those two are after me? Like I said, this whole thing is going to be a cinch." Frankie twirled around and skated toward the center of the floor. He was a good skater, fast and sure of himself.

Travis felt a tap on his shoulder. It was Annie. "I've been looking everywhere for you," she said. "Where have you been?"

"Right here." Travis stared. Beside Annie stood her little brother, Reed, and some girl with short blond hair who looked a lot like Penelope Finchester.

"Hi, Travis, Hi, Marcus," said the girl. "Have you seen Frankie?"

It was Penelope. She had on tight blue jeans and a fuzzy yellow sweater and hoop earrings. With short hair Penelope Finchester was almost pretty.

She laughed. "What's wrong with you two? I got my hair cut, okay? You're looking at me like I'm on the endangered species list."

"It's just that you look so different tonight," said Marcus.

"Yeah," said Travis, "We didn't know you without your buttons."

Annie glared at him.

"I've never been to a skating party before," said Penelope. "This looks like fun."

"Only if you like girls," said Reed. "I hate them." He was wearing his usual outfit, drooping jeans, a white T-shirt, empty eyeglass frames and a tattered Superman's cape. Ever since he'd seen his first Superman movie on television, Reed had been crazy about the man from Krypton. Some days he wore his glass frames and pretended to be Clark Kent, the mild-mannered reporter. Other days he ran around in the red cape with an *S* on the back that his grandmother had made, pretending to be Superman.

Reed looked at the older kids skating around them. "Superman doesn't roller-skate, he flies from place to place," said Reed. He held out his arms as if he were going to take off.

"Keep your glasses on," said Annie. "I don't want you flying around here all night."

The lights softened and the music slowed. "Tonight's first couples-skate will be a ladies' choice, a ladies' choice," said the disc jockey. "Choose your partners, girls."

"Annie, I'm hungry," said Reed.

"Not now," said Annie, "this is a ladies' choice."

"I don't want to skate with you," said Reed. "I only skate with Lois Lane."

"I didn't ask you," said Annie. "Here's some money, go get something to eat."

Reed skated off toward the snack bar.

Annie turned toward Travis and Marcus. "Would you like to skate with me?" she asked.

"Sure," said Travis. He started to take her hand but she pulled away. "I was talking to Marcus," said Annie. She tilted her head toward Penelope. Oh! He was supposed to skate with Penelope, he realized.

Annie took Marcus's hand and pulled him toward the other couples already in motion around the floor. "Come on, Marcus. Let's go."

"All right," said Marcus, "but I'm not real good at this, yet."

Travis watched as Marcus wobbled out toward the floor holding tightly to Annie's hand.

In the center of the floor, a half dozen girls crowded around Frankie, but he ignored them. He was waving at Penelope and motioning for her to come over.

"I guess that leaves the two of us. Would you like to skate with me, Travis?" asked Penelope. If she saw Frankie waving she pretended not to.

Travis looked at her. "Me? You want to skate with me?"

"Sure." She dabbed at her red nose and watery eyes with a lace handkerchief then stuffed it into her pocket. "As long as you understand I'm not very good at this either."

Travis followed her onto the floor. They skated past Marcus who was edging inch by inch along the railing while Annie skated slowly beside him.

"Come on, Marcus, let go of the railing," said Annie. "You'll never learn to skate that way."

"Don't rush me," said Marcus. "I like to take my time at these things."

Travis nodded to a few of the kids as they skated by. They're looking at me strangely, he thought. Probably because I'm skating with the school geek.

"You're really good at this," Penelope said. "Do you give lessons?" She tightened her grip on his hand so she wouldn't fall.

Travis smiled. The colored lights made Penelope's short blond hair sparkle in the darkened room and he realized that if he didn't know Penelope, he might think she was kind of cute.

"You know, Annie was right," said Penelope.

"How's that?"

"She told me skating was a lot like basketball. You just have to practice," she said.

Travis skated slowly trying to match his movements to hers. "How do you like managing the team?" he asked.

Penelope shrugged. "I like it okay. I really wanted to play," she said. "But during tryouts, I was terrible. I couldn't dribble or shoot. Annie tried to teach me, but I was hopeless." Penelope laughed a little. "Mrs. Klein knew I wanted to be part of the team so she chose me as the team manager."

Reed stood behind the railing eating cotton candy. He still had on his empty frames. Travis waved to Clark Kent as they skated past.

"What about you? Do you like basketball?" asked Penelope.

"If you're a friend of Annie's, you have to like it," said Travis. "It's required."

Penelope nodded. "I think Annie's the best player on the whole team, maybe in the whole school."

"I agree," said Travis. "But don't tell Frankie that, he thinks he's the star player at King."

Penelope frowned. "I know he talks that way, but once you get to know him, you find out he's a great guy."

Travis looked at her. Was she talking about the same Frankie Murphy he knew?

"In fact," she continued, "up until about a week ago, I thought he was stuck on himself. But now I've gotten a chance to really know him." She smiled. "I found out that we're a lot alike."

"You and Frankie? How?" This was something Travis wanted to hear.

"Well," said Penelope, "we both love the color blue, and we both eat Oreo cookies by opening them up and licking off the icing first."

"Oh, sure," said Travis, "that makes you almost identical twins."

Penelope laughed. "It's not just that. Frankie and I are both kind of shy and have trouble talking to other people."

Travis glanced over his shoulder. Frankie was skating with a large group of girls trailing after him. "Funny, he doesn't look shy."

"With most people, I don't know what to say, but with Frankie I can—" She stopped. Allison and Mollie skated up beside them.

"Penelope," said Mollie, "what did you do to your hair? I just love it."

"I got it cut today," said Penelope.

"It looks wonderful," said Allison. "Has Frankie seen it yet?"

Penelope shook her head. "I don't think so. I think he's skating with somebody else."

"We know," said Mollie. "He's skating with that Terry Hays. She's such a flirt and so pushy. She practically ran over me trying to get to Frankie first." Mollie patted her curly hair. "I just can't stand girls who chase after boys like that, can you?"

"Hey, Penelope!" yelled Frankie, "Save the next couples-skate for me, will you?" Frankie reached out and punched Travis's arm as he skated by. "What are you trying to do, Marshall, mess things up for me?"

"Now, now, boys, let's not fight over Penelope." Mollie yelled. "I'm sure she'll have time to skate with both of you. You just have to take turns."

Penelope's face turned pink and she looked down at the floor.

Frankie repeated his question. "How about it, Penelope, are you going to skate with me or not?"

Without taking her eyes off the toes of her skates, Penelope nodded.

"Okay, next couples-skate then." Frankie skated faster and Terry Hays and six other girls hurried after him. "Hear that, Marshall?" called Frankie over his shoulder. "Next couples-skate, be there."

Mollie and Allison looked at Frankie and then back at Travis. "We think there is something going on around here that we should know about," said Mollie.

Travis held tightly to Penelope's small soft hand and skated away.

They circled the floor together without saying a word. I shouldn't have made such a big deal about her being the first on Frankie's list, thought Travis. She really likes that jerk, and she thinks he likes her too.

The silver globe overhead sent streams of red and blue light shining down on the couples skating around the floor. Penelope touched Travis's sleeve and the circles of golden light floated over her fingertips. "Your jacket is really soft," she said. "I like it."

"Thanks," said Travis. Annie's right, he thought, Penelope really is a nice girl once you get to know her.

"Frankie says he's going to get one just like it."

The slow music faded. "It's limbo time!" announced the roller rink disc jockey. "Anyone who wants to limbo, come out to the floor and form a straight line!"

Penelope let go of Travis's hand. "Thanks for skating with me. I'll see you later." Travis watched as she skated toward the center of the floor where people were lining up into one long line for the limbo contest.

Looking around the room, Travis saw Annie standing at the snack bar with Reed. He glided over and stopped between them. "Do you want to skate the next couples-skate with me?" he asked.

"I'll skate with you," said Reed.

"I didn't ask you," said Travis, "I asked your sister."

Annie took a sip of soda and eyed him. "Why did Marcus come to the skating party tonight?"

"What do you mean?"

"He's never come before," said Annie. "He can't even skate."

Travis shrugged. "I don't know. Maybe it's because it's the last skating party we'll have before we go to junior high school and he wanted to see what it was like."

Annie glanced over at Marcus who was leaning against a wall, working with his calculator. "I asked him about why he came, and he gave me this big story about this being part of his science project. He said he was studying the moon's gravitational pull on people who skate on circular floors under electric lights."

Gravitational pull under electric lights? Give me a break! thought Travis. Marcus should have told Annie that he wanted to learn how to skate.

Annie stabbed the ice in the bottom of her cup with a straw. "If you ask me, there's something strange going on here tonight. I don't like it."

Travis shoved his hands into the pockets of his jacket. The list was still there. He decided to change the subject. "Annie, why did you ask Marcus to skate instead of me?" he asked. "You know we always skate together, the first couples-skate."

"I know," said Annie. She took a long drink of soda. "We do a lot of things together, but I'm not sure I like it."

"What do you mean?"

"I mean that sometimes I'd like you to ask me. You know, treat me like a real girl and not one of the guys."

"Yeah, but to me you are like one of the guys. After all, you've been my best friend since we were little kids."

"I know," said Annie, "but sometimes, I'd like

you to think of me as a—" her voice trailed off.

Loud music over the speaker signaled the end of the limbo contest and skaters again circled the rink, sometimes alone, sometimes in pairs. Tony Foley and Johnny Watson were playing tag on skates until the manager, a blond fat man in red skates, pulled them over for going too fast.

"Couples-skate next," said the announcer. "Boys, ask a partner. It's couples-skate time."

"Ah, not again," yelled Reed. "All people do around here is talk and couples-skate. This is dumb." He pulled a piece of red licorice out of his pocket. The licorice looked as if somebody had skated over it. He took a bite. "You two go ahead, I'm going to eat this one out."

Holding on to the outer railing, Marcus edged his way toward them. "Hey, Travis, take me out there. It's time."

Annie moved backward to make room for Marcus. "I don't get it," she said. "Are you skating with him or me?"

"I'm skating with you." Travis took her hand and led her toward the floor and the other couples. Marcus skated behind them holding on to the railing.

Travis spotted Frankie. He had his arm around Penelope's shoulders and was guiding her around the rink. Frankie turned and smiled at Travis, motioning for him to come closer.

Travis skated faster to catch up, but Annie shook her head and pulled him back. "Let's stay back here. I don't want to be near that creep tonight."

Frankie and Penelope circled the rink once. The lights were turned down low and the music from the loud speaker was soft and dreamy. Couples skated past them, some of them dancing.

Travis and Annie matched each other's movements with a slow easy rhythm. They had learned to skate at this rink. Every Saturday during third grade, Annie's mother would drop the two of them off at the rink.

Frankie appeared at Travis's side and elbowed his way in front of him. Annie slowed but Travis stumbled then caught himself by grasping the railing.

"Hey, what's going on?" yelled Annie. "Watch where you're going. You almost tripped us."

Frankie appeared not to hear. Instead, he pulled Penelope closer.

It would be any second now, thought Travis. The song was almost over.

Tony and Allison skated up beside them.

Travis watched. What's he waiting for, wondered Travis, a drum roll?

Frankie held up one finger and looked down at

Penelope. Then slowly and carefully, so that everybody behind him could see, he leaned over and kissed her. It was a long, hard kiss right on the mouth.

"Yuck!" said Annie. "What is that creep doing?"

"He kissed her," screamed Mollie. "Frankie Murphy kissed Penelope!"

Penelope pulled away, confused and embarrassed. Her gold earrings bobbed in the darkness. Murmurs from people around her were loud and clear.

"He kissed her. Did you see it? Frankie kissed Penelope."

The music ended and the lights came up. It was break time. The disc jockey climbed out of the booth and headed toward the back office.

Frankie let go of Penelope's hand, leaving her alone and partnerless on the floor. He skated over to Travis and whispered in his ear, "One down and six to go," and then glided away.

An instant later, he was skating with Terry Hays. Smiling, talking, he grabbed her hand and pulled her toward the snack bar. Terry laughed. Her red hair was decorated with two blue barrettes. As everyone watched they skated toward the back booth.

Annie skated over to Penelope. "Come on, Penelope, let's go to the girls' room."

Travis realized what was going to happen next. When two sixth-grade girls headed for the ladies' room it could only mean one thing . . . one of them was going to cry.

Travis was surrounded by Marcus and a gang of sixth-grade boys. With great formality, Marcus took the list from his coat pocket and unfolded it. Taking a pen from his plastic pocket protector, he drew a line through Penelope's name. "Well, that takes care of Finchester," said Marcus. "She's off the list. Check her off yours too."

Reed skated up to them. His glasses were off now and his cape was flying. "Hey, what's going on? Why is Penelope crying? Did she fall?"

"You could say that," said Marcus with a smirk. He folded the list and put it back into his pocket.

Tony skated up to the crowd around Travis and Marcus. "I think you should cross off Terry Hays," he said. "She and Frankie are in that last booth over there and she's laughing like crazy. I think he's going to kiss her tonight too."

"Go back over and mill around," instructed Marcus. "He has to do it in front of somebody or it won't be legal."

Travis pulled his *A*'s jacket around him. He felt a little guilty. No, more than a little guilty. Something wasn't right about this. He grabbed Marcus's arm. "What about Penelope?"

"What about her?"

"I mean, what will happen to her? She doesn't understand any of this."

"Of course not," said Marcus, "none of the girls does. That's part of the deal."

"But it doesn't seem fair. I mean, she may have been embarrassed about him kissing her in front of everybody like that."

Marcus shrugged. "She'll get over it."

"But she thought Frankie liked her," said Travis. "He just skated away from her without saying anything. And now she's in the bathroom crying."

"So?" said Marcus. "Why do you care? You said yourself she's weird."

"But that was before . . ."

"Before what?"

"Before I got to know her."

Tony rolled out of the snack bar holding up two fingers. Marcus reached into his pocket for the list. "Would you look at that? Murphy kissed another one. The guy is amazing." Marcus crossed out Terry's name with a flourish and checked his watch.

"If he keeps going like this, he'll kiss three or four more before this party's over."

Reed tugged at Travis's sleeve. "What's going on? Why is Frankie Murphy kissing everybody?" said Reed. He had on his glasses now.

Marcus leaned down and looked at Reed. "What's with the empty glass frames?"

"He thinks he's Clark Kent," explained Travis. "When he wears those glasses he can't fly."

"Fly? He thinks he can fly?" Marcus looked Reed in the eye. "Look, kid, this is none of your business. And if you know what's good for you, you won't tell anybody about what you heard here tonight, especially your sister."

Reed took off his glasses. "You can't scare Superman," he said. "I'm indivisible."

"Indivisible? You can't be divided. What's that supposed to mean?" said Marcus.

The disc jockey carried a cup of coffee back into the music booth. In a few seconds loud rock music poured over the loudspeaker.

Annie came out of no-man's-land, without Penelope.

"Where's that creep Frankie Murphy?" yelled Annie. "I want to find him and tell him what I think of him."

"You can't do that," said Travis.

"Who says? Penelope is in there crying her eyes out because of him."

"Well, she didn't have to kiss him."

"You saw it! He kissed *her*. Besides, no one had ever kissed her before. She didn't know what to do."

"Well, she didn't try to stop him."

Annie looked at him. "Travis, whose side are you on, anyway?"

"Yours, I mean Penelope's," said Travis. "But I thought she should have put up more of a fight. You would have."

"You saw it, that creep kissed her and then skated away," said Annie.

"I would have crushed his legs into molten steel," said Reed. "That's what Superman does when people kiss him."

"Be quiet, Reed," said Annie, "this is important stuff."

"What's so important about Frankie kissing people?"

Over the loudspeaker came the disc jockey's voice. "Last skate, everyone, thanks for coming to the Flying Wheels Roller Rink. We'll see you again next week." He turned up the volume of the music. "Now, everybody out on the floor!"

Travis took Reed's and Annie's hands, "Come on, let's skate this last one together."

"I have my glasses," said Reed. "I can't fly."

Annie looked around the rink. "I'm still not through with that slimeball Frankie Murphy. When I tell all the girls on the team what he did to Penelope, they are going to be really mad."

Good, thought Travis to himself. There are five girls left and three of them are on the basketball team. When they hear how Frankie treated Penelope, there's no way they'll even speak to the guy. Travis smiled. Good going, Murphy, he thought. There's no way you can win the bet now!

five

The warm May evening smelled sweet and fresh. Travis waited outside St. Mary's Church for Marcus. He held on to his clarinet case and looked around. He had just finished playing at the church concert. It was St. Mary's annual church carnival and practically the whole town was there.

As he leaned against the church wall, Travis watched the grown-ups play bingo and the teenagers walk by holding hands. Small children darted back and forth between the carnival games and the food stalls while their parents waited, holding jackets and half-eaten hot dogs.

In the corner booth the members of the church auxiliary sold homemade cakes and plates of chocolate fudge. The church parking lot was filled with the glow of colored lights and the smell of fresh popcorn.

It had been a whole week since the roller skating party at the Flying Wheels Roller Rink. A whole week of everybody talking about how Frankie had kissed Penelope Finchester and Terry Hays on the very same night. A whole week when the entire girls' basketball team hissed at Frankie every time he came within six feet of them.

On Monday and Tuesday after the skating party, Penelope wasn't at school. When Annie called, Mrs. Finchester told her Penelope was down with her allergies. Annie didn't believe it and neither did Travis.

On Wednesday, Penelope was back in the art room as if nothing had happened. This time she was making buttons for the St. Mary's building fund. Church officials hoped to build a new youth center in the open field next to the parking lot. Since Annie attended St. Mary's, she joined Penelope in her button-making.

The two of them had set up a table downstairs in the church basement with the arts and crafts booths. Annie told Travis they had made over a hundred colored buttons that said ST. MARY'S: BUILD-ING WITH LOVE AND LUMBER.

Travis decided to steer clear of the two button sellers until he'd met with Marcus.

At exactly seven o'clock the Turnby station wagon rolled into the church parking lot. Mr. Turnby, like Marcus, was always punctual. He stopped the car and Marcus got out carrying a long cardboard box.

"I'll pick you up at precisely nine o'clock, Marcus." Mr. Turnby pointed at Travis's clarinet case. "Are you playing tonight, Travis?"

"I already did. The concert is over," said Travis.

"Too bad we missed it. Have a good time, boys." Mr. Turnby waved at them and drove off.

"What's in the box?" said Travis.

"You'll see," said Marcus. "Where's Frankie?"

"Frankie? I didn't know he was coming."

Marcus gave him an exasperated look, "Of course he's coming. Why do you think I called and asked you to meet me here? I wouldn't spend a Friday night at a carnival if I didn't have to."

If Frankie was coming tonight and Marcus was here, Travis realized, it must have something to do with the bet and the list.

Marcus checked his watch. "He said he would meet us here at seven o'clock and it's already 7:02." Marcus looked around the parking lot. "I had to rush through dinner, just to get here on time. And we were having my favorite—pizza with anchovies." He shifted the long box to his other arm. "He'd better show up soon or I'm going home."

Tony popped out from behind a nearby honeysuckle bush. He was wearing sunglasses and what looked like his father's trench coat.

"Nice coat," said Marcus. "Is it going to rain or are you meeting the FBI later?"

Tony peered over his dark glasses without smiling.

"Where's Frankie?" asked Marcus.

"He'll be here later. He's setting things up." Tony paused and pointed at the box. "Is that it?"

Marcus held up the box. "Just like you ordered."

"Now, do you remember what to do?"

Marcus nodded. "Of course, the instructions were simple. We're to wait for Frankie to get on the Ferris wheel and then let three seats pass by us before getting on too."

"Yeah, but don't make a big deal of it," said Tony. "We don't want to mess this up."

"What do you mean?" said Travis.

Tony lowered his voice. "The bet is supposed to be secret, remember? If any of the girls find out what Frankie's planning tonight, it will blow the whole thing."

Tony checked his watch and then looked up at the sky. "It's getting dark, come on." Signaling the boys to follow him, Tony made his way through the crowd toward the carnival rides.

At the edge of an open field, a sign announced the building site of St. Mary's new church hall. Off to the right, as far as Travis could see, were game booths and carnival rides. As the boys made their way through the crowds, men in sleeveless shirts with tattoos on their arms called out to them, "Come on, boys, take a chance. Win a prize for your sweetie."

Each man urged them to step closer, spin a wheel, throw a ball and win, win, win. But the boys pushed forward toward the Ferris wheel.

On the other side of the carnival games were the rides. Mothers and toddlers listened to loud calliope music as they waited their turn to go on a beat-up merry-go-round of wild-looking horses that galloped up and down.

Parents with video cameras filmed their children circling the track in miniature cars or sailing by in miniature boats. Six tired ponies trotted around a well-worn circle carrying children wearing cowboy hats.

Tony pointed to the rides for older children. "Over there," he said.

Long lines of children were waiting to take spins in the Barrel of Fun or swing in the one-hundred-foot aerial glider swing or scream their guts out on the Green Hornet roller coaster. Past these rides and several others stood the Ferris wheel.

Tony dropped into a crouch and whispered, "Stay down, so they don't see us."

"Who's they?" asked Travis.

"Quiet," whispered Tony. "This is no time for questions." Tony crept across the field toward the lights of the Ferris wheel. Marcus hunkered down, too, dragging along the cardboard box.

Travis shifted his clarinet case to the other hand and then strolled up to the long line for the Ferris wheel.

Frankie Murphy was standing at the front of the line talking to Ricky Romer and Katy O'Donnel.

Marcus was counting the people in front of them, "This isn't right, we're too far back. We've got to be three seats behind them to make this thing work."

"It's handled," said Tony. "My cousin is up ahead holding our place. Let Frankie and the girls get on first and then we'll move up."

At the controls of the Ferris wheel stood a fat man in a greasy sweatshirt. With his right hand he moved a metal lever, and the wooden seat glided slowly to a stop.

Travis watched Frankie and the two girls walk up the short wooden ramp and take a seat. Frankie took out a string of tickets and handed three to the man.

"You got a lot of tickets there, kid. You going to ride all night?"

"Maybe," said Frankie. "What's it to you?"

"Smart-aleck kid," the man mumbled, as he slammed the steel bar into place locking Frankie and Katy and Ricky into the chair.

Frankie leaned backward, making the seat sway to and fro. The girls laughed nervously.

"Don't rock the chair, kid," yelled the man. "Just sit there and ride the ride."

Frankie slid an arm around each of the girls. He gave the man one of his big Hollywood smiles.

The man pulled the lever and lowered the next chair as Frankie and the girls moved up and away.

Travis and the others slipped forward in line

beside Tony's cousin. "Wait a minute," said Marcus, "we didn't buy any tickets."

The cousin smiled and pulled a wad of tickets from his pocket. "It's covered. Frankie told me to get them. You owe me five bucks apiece." Two more people took a seat and the Ferris wheel moved again. Tony's cousin waved good-bye and meandered off into the night.

An old man and a little boy got on next.

"Wait a minute," said Travis, "five bucks for one ride?"

"Three rides for five dollars," said Tony. "If it doesn't work the first time, we have orders to sit tight and do it again."

The man moved the Ferris wheel with the lever.

"Do what again?" said Travis.

"You'll see," said Tony. "Come on, it's our turn." He walked up the wooden ramp and sat down. Travis followed.

"What's in the case, kid?" said the man.

"My clarinet."

"You thinking of playing up there?"

"No," said Travis. "It was for the church concert. I already played."

"Good thing," said the man. "People don't like noise when they're riding my ride."

The man glared at Marcus. "I don't have all day, kid. Are you coming or not?"

Marcus slid the box under one arm and walked up the ramp. "I hate heights," mumbled Marcus. "Being up high makes me feel out of control."

The man laughed. "You ain't seen nothing, yet. Wait till you're four hundred feet in the air." The man pointed at the box Marcus was holding. "What's in this one?"

Marcus was looking up at the top of the wheel.

"If that's full of water balloons, you can get off right now," said the man. "I don't want no water balloons on my Ferris wheel."

"This? Oh, this is part of a science fair project," said Marcus. "I'm trying to decipher the number of times a Ferris wheel rotates within a six-minute ride and how it contributes to the problem of global warming."

The man smiled showing tobacco-stained teeth. "You know, I used to like that science stuff when I was a kid. I was always making smoke bombs, lighting firecrackers, stuff like that. How many minutes do you gotta be up there to make it work?"

"Six," said Marcus.

"You got it, kid." The man pulled the safety bar across them and the chair jerked upward.

Marcus looked down to make sure the man still had his hand on the lever. "I don't know why Frankie has to use a Ferris wheel. This whole thing could have been done just as easily on the merry-go-round."

The chair moved slowly up into the night sky, stopping and starting so that people below could get on and off the ride.

High above the carnival grounds, Travis dared himself to look down. The people below looked small and far away, like ants scurrying about under a giant flashlight.

When the ride was filled, the Ferris wheel began to pick up speed. For a while, things felt fine. The warm spring air, the smell of popcorn, the distant sound of the calliope, made Travis feel better. In a few weeks, school will be out, he thought. Summer will be here, and he and Annie would go swimming, ride bikes, and play baseball. For a while Travis forgot why he was there and enjoyed the ride as the Ferris wheel went up, around, and down toward the ground again.

Tony took off his sunglasses. "Now that we're moving, let's get things set up."

"What things?" said Travis. "I don't get it. What are we supposed to be doing here?"

"It's simple," said Marcus. "By my calculations a six-minute ride will give us nine complete turns on the wheel before Mr. Wizard, down there, begins to slow the ride and people disembark."

"He means get off the ride," Tony said.

"I know what disembark means," Travis said.

In the glow of the Ferris wheel lights, Marcus's face was a sickly shade of green. He swallowed twice and continued. "As people get off, each seat on the Ferris wheel will remain on top for exactly forty-nine seconds." Marcus gave Travis a weak smile.

"Are you telling me he's going to kiss those girls while they're trapped on the top of a Ferris wheel?"

"Great idea, isn't it?" said Tony. "The boy's a genius."

"No fair!" said Travis. "There's got to be a witness. If he kisses them on top of the wheel, nobody can see it."

Tony smiled. "Show him what's in the box, Einstein."

Marcus lifted the lid of the box. Inside, covered with tissue paper, were two small mirrors attached to a long thin tube.

"What is it?" asked Travis.

"What's it look like?"

Travis touched the long metal tube. The mirrors at each end could be tilted in various directions. "Search me."

"It's a periscope," said Marcus. "I built it myself."

Travis looked at him.

"He still doesn't get it," said Tony. "Show him."

Marcus took the periscope out of the box and adjusted the mirrors. He held one end up to his eye.

Tony leaned backward in the chair.

"Hey, who's tilting the chair?" said Marcus. "Keep it still, will you?"

"Hurry up and get them into view," said Tony. "We've got one more spin around and then it will be time to get off this thing."

Marcus fiddled with the top of the tube, turning the mirror this way, then that.

The Ferris wheel slowed to a stop. Down below, the man was letting people off the ride. Travis looked up. They were sitting in a chair just four stops from the very top.

"Here," said Marcus, "take a look." He handed the periscope to Travis. "You have a clear shot of what's going on in Frankie's chair."

Holding the periscope straight up, Travis put his eye at one end and looked through. "I can't see anything. It's all dark."

"Turn it more to the left," said Marcus. He stopped and looked down at the ground. "Wow, we're really up high."

"They're not doing anything," said Travis. "He's just talking to them."

"He's setting them up for the kill," whispered Tony. "The guy's a genius." The chair rocked backward and Marcus grabbed onto the safety bar with both hands. "Whoever's rocking this chair, better stop it!"

Travis closed one eye and peered into the tube. "It's perfect. I can see all three of them." The chair rocked forward.

"Hey," said Marcus, "I told you, don't do that. When we sway like that, it makes me sick!" Marcus closed his eyes and leaned back holding on to the safety bar.

Tony laughed. "Come on, Marcus, you're not afraid of a little swinging, are you? What do you say we bounce this baby and see how it feels?" Tony stomped his feet and the chair swung back and forth.

"Don't," said Marcus. Travis could see beads of sweat forming on Marcus's forehead as he death-gripped the safety bar. "Maybe I shouldn't have eaten all that pizza tonight," mumbled Marcus. "I don't feel that good."

Tony stood up and leaned forward so the chair swung out and over the people waiting below.

"Tony, sit down, will you?" screamed Travis.

"I'm not kidding," said Marcus. "The motion of this thing makes me sick."

Tony looked up. "Quick, get the scope, they're at the top!"

six

Later, after Travis had helped Marcus off the Ferris wheel and called Mr. Turnby, after he and the Ferris wheel man cleaned up the seat and wrapped up the periscope, after he saw Frankie and agreed that he'd seen two kisses, Travis washed off his clarinet case and went to find Annie and Penelope.

The arts and crafts booths were set up in the church basement. It was a large cavernous room with tables stacked high with pillows, pot holders, flowered wreaths, and dolls made out of mop handles. Travis saw Penelope at once. She was seated next to a woman who was selling handbags made out of old inner tubes. It looked as if Penelope and the woman were trying to fasten crushed beer cans together and fashion them into hats. Penelope looked up and smiled. The table was filled with yellow buttons. "Where have you been?" asked Penelope. "You're as white as a ghost."

Travis nodded and sat down beside her. He picked up one of the yellow buttons and examined it. It said ST. MARY'S BUILDING FUND. So much had happened, even if he could tell her, he wouldn't know how. In one night, Frankie had checked two girls off the list. By last count there was only Mollie, Allison, and Annie left. Things didn't look good.

"Were you over at the rides?" asked Penelope.

Travis nodded. "I rode the Ferris wheel for a little while. It makes me sick sometimes."

Penelope nodded sympathetically. "Annie went on home," she said. "We weren't selling many buttons so I told her there was no use both of us sitting here."

Travis wanted to see Annie, but he didn't want to leave Penelope alone. He still felt responsible about what had happened at the roller rink.

"You don't have to stay if you don't want to," she said. "I'm okay. In fact, being here tonight gives me lots of new ideas. See those hats over there?" She pointed to another table a few feet away. On each hat was a pair of big brown antlers designed to make the wearer look like a bull moose in early spring. "I was thinking," said Penelope, "of making baseball caps for each endangered animal. I could make one with little pointed ears for the wolf or add a long trunk for the African elephant."

Travis nodded trying to imagine himself wearing a baseball cap that made him look like a passenger on Noah's ark. "I like the *A's*," he said, pointing to his jacket. "Most people wear sports teams on their heads."

"Well, what about this?" Penelope held up a beer can hat. "People who like sports drink beer."

"You can say that again," said the woman with the inner tube handbags. "My husband drinks a six-pack every time the Raiders play."

Penelope spread glue on the back of the can. "People could wear their favorite beer can on their head and clean up the environment at the same time."

The woman nodded. "Sounds good to me."

Travis stood up. "I don't think so, Penelope. Most parents are not going to let a kid wear a beer can on his head."

"Maybe you're right." Penelope tossed the beer

can on the table. "I'll just have to think of something else."

Travis started to put back the button he was holding. "No," said Penelope. "Take it. It's on the house for all your advice."

"I didn't do anything, I just told you what I would wear."

"Not just that," said Penelope. "When you warned me about Frankie Murphy. You were right."

"I just didn't want you to get hurt."

"I guess I made a fool of myself, didn't I?"

"No, you didn't," said Travis.

"I don't know why I thought somebody like Frankie Murphy would like me." She tried to smile. "I guess I acted like a real jerk."

"Don't say that," insisted Travis. "The only jerk last week was Murphy. You didn't do anything to feel bad about. If anybody was to blame, it was me."

"What do you mean?"

"I mean that—that—" he stammered, trying to find the right words. "Forget about Frankie, Penelope. You're a nice girl even if you do have some crazy ideas about what people should wear on their heads."

Penelope laughed.

Just then a woman and a set of twins stepped up to Penelope's table and began looking at the array of buttons.

Penelope turned toward the customers and Travis left.

Later, when Travis got to Annie's house, Reed was out in the front yard with a flashlight, running back and forth between the front porch and the gate, searching for something. He had on his pajama bottoms and his Superman cape.

"What are you looking for?" asked Travis.

Reed didn't answer. He made flying noises as he ran by.

"Is Annie home?"

Reed ignored him. His eyes were fixed on the ground as he ran back and forth over the same part of the yard.

From out back, Travis heard the sound of someone playing basketball behind the garage. He opened the gate to go in.

"Halt, earthman!" yelled Reed. "You can't get through this way, I've got my radon force shield up. You'll die if you enter here."

"Come on, Reed, I want to go out back and see Annie. I can hear she's back there."

"Go around." He pointed to the alley. "I'm looking for the house key and you might step on it in the dark."

"Don't tell me you lost another house key."

Reed nodded.

"Why don't you wait till morning and look for the key then? You can see better in the light."

"Superman can't sleep when the house key is lost," yelled Reed. "Robbers might find it. And then, tonight when we're asleep, they'll unlock the door and get us!" He pushed back his thick blond hair and stared down at the grass. "Besides, Mom is going to be really mad at me if I don't find it."

Travis walked around the flashlight beam toward the back of the house. Annie's father had put up a basketball hoop on the side of the garage the year they were all in third grade. Last year he'd added ground lines and a string of lightbulbs so she could play at night.

Annie was under the hoop practicing her dunk shots. "Hey, how you doing?" she said. "Want to shoot some?"

"No," said Travis, "I have to get on home." He watched her put one shot up and in with her left hand. Annie dribbled the ball toward center court. "I was just over at St. Mary's," said Travis. "I talked to Penelope and she said you went on home."

"Yeah, I was there for a little while, but Mom had

to go out and I'm baby-sitting Reed." She stood at center court and shot a three pointer. "He's still out in the front, isn't he?"

Travis nodded. He put his clarinet case down on the ground. "I played at the St. Mary's concert and then I went to the carnival."

"Was it fun?"

"It was okay."

"You don't look so good," said Annie. "Are you all right?"

"The Ferris wheel. It makes me sick sometimes."

Annie nodded and bounced the ball again. For a moment, she concentrated on the basket, then made her throw. The ball went up and over and through the steel rim as if there were a magnet inside. "So, are you going to Mollie's birthday party tomorrow?" she asked.

Travis nodded. "That's why I stopped by. I thought we could go over there together. I haven't been over to Mollie's since the fourth grade when she had that swimming party for the class, remember?"

"Do I remember, you practically drowned that day, showing off in front of Allison and Mollie. Good thing I was there to pull you out."

"Yep," agreed Travis. "You've saved my neck lots of times, haven't you?"

"Yep, that's why we're best friends, right?"

Out front Reed was making loud flying noises, ZOOM, ZOOM, ZOOM! And for a moment Travis wished that he were Reed's age again—six years old when he and Annie played *Star Wars*. They used to take turns playing Han Solo and Luke Skywalker. Annie wouldn't be Princess Leia because all she did in the movie was get kidnapped and rescued. Things were easier back then, Travis thought.

"Is something bothering you?" Annie asked.

Travis stared at their shadows on the garage wall. The lights above the court made dark outlines of a short round body next to Annie's tall, thin one. "Frankie Murphy was there tonight with Ricky Romer and Katy O'Donnel," said Travis.

Annie made a face to show how she felt about any information concerning Frankie Murphy.

"When they were on the top of the Ferris wheel, he was rocking the chair like crazy and both girls were hollering their heads off. He kissed them."

"How do you know?"

"I saw it through Marcus's periscope."

"You took a periscope on the Ferris wheel? Why?"

"It's a long story." Travis hesitated, trying to phrase the next question just right. "Would you do that?" he asked.

"I don't know. I don't have a periscope."

"No, I mean kiss Frankie Murphy?"

She threw the basketball at him. "Who wants to know?"

Travis caught it with both hands. "Come on, tell me. If he wanted you to, would you ever kiss him or not?"

Annie grabbed her throat and made a gagging sound.

Travis waited for a real answer.

"Kiss old pumpkin-head Murphy? No way. I'd die first."

Good, thought Travis. "Yeah, but the guy's sneaky. And sometimes people can end up kissing without really wanting to."

"How?"

"Oh, you know, by accident. Like you could both be coming around the same corner and sort of bump into each other and end up kissing."

Annie laughed and shook her head. "That's not kissing, that's hit and run." She stepped closer. "The way I see it, you either kiss somebody or you don't." Her voice was serious. "Besides, if I ever did kiss anyone, I would want to kiss somebody I really liked. Somebody I'd known for a while."

"Me too." And with those words, Travis felt his

face turn a deep red. Annie seemed different tonight and, for some reason, he didn't know what to do or say next.

"Annie!" It was Reed, holding on to his pajama bottoms as he ran. "Annie, you got to help me find the house key," he yelled. "Mom is going to kill me if I don't find it."

Annie took the basketball from Travis and tucked it under her arm. "He's right, she will kill him. It's the third key he's lost this month." Annie picked up her sweatshirt and handed it to her little brother. "You shouldn't be out here in just your PJ's. Put this on."

"I've got my cape," said Reed. "Superman is made of steel and never gets cold."

Annie handed Travis his clarinet case then walked over to the side of the garage and turned off the lights. The three of them stood there for a moment letting their eyes adjust to the dark.

"Do you want to stay for a while? I have to put Reed to bed in a few minutes and then we could talk." She pointed to the clarinet. "Or maybe you could give me a private concert."

"I want to hear Travis play too," said Reed. "I want him to teach me something on the clarinet."

"Not tonight," said Travis, "I'd better be going."

He didn't feel like playing and the idea of being alone with Annie made him feel guilty.

"Pick me up tomorrow and we'll walk to Mollie's house together. Okay?" She punched him softly in the arm. "And don't worry so much about Murphy. Like I said before, I think that guy is a real jerk."

seven

It was after three o'clock by the time Annie and Travis arrived at Mollie Sherman's birthday party. The oak trees along the driveway leading up to the house were decorated with pink balloons and yellow streamers.

All the guests were in the backyard. Small tables with wooden folding chairs were arranged around the yard and under a large yellow tent. Serving people in white uniforms were passing silver trays laden with bite-size pieces of food.

Mollie's parents and relatives stood about talking and laughing together; the party was well under way.

At the edge of the yard, next to the swimming pool, sat Allison, Mollie, Marcus, and Frankie. Both boys wore dark suits, but Frankie was wearing a soft pink shirt and a bright yellow tie. His curly black hair was combed back making him look much older than the others.

Frankie let out a deep low whistle. "Hey, Davis, you look great! You should wear a dress more often."

Annie's face turned the same color as the punch. For a moment, Travis couldn't tell if she was going to thank Frankie or hit him. Then she smiled. She likes it, thought Travis. She liked his whistling at her. One more reason to hate Frankie Murphy.

"It's about time you two got here," said Mollie. "We've been waiting for you." She was in a yellow dress with a pink sash at the waist. Her long red hair was piled on top of her head and tied with pink and yellow ribbons. And she was wearing rose-colored lipstick and pale green eyeshadow.

"Doesn't everything look just perfect?" said Allison. She motioned toward the tables covered with pink and yellow tablecloths and baskets of pink and yellow flowers.

"Pink and yellow are my favorite colors," announced Mollie. "My mother told the caterer that we had to have everything in pink and yellow."

Marcus studied the glass of punch he was holding. "The pink is okay, but these yellow ice cubes look like little frozen egg yolks."

"They do not," said Allison. "I think yellow ice cubes are absolutely perfect. When I have my birthday party I want yellow ice cubes too."

A man in a yellow shirt and a little green hat began to play the accordion.

Mollie shrugged. "I asked my mother for a band but she said I was too young. Besides, my cousin Seymour said he'd play for free."

"I think accordion music is just perfect," said Allison. "When I have my birthday party, I'm definitely having an accordion player."

Everyone stood for a few moments without saying anything, listening to Cousin Seymour's accordion version of "Rock Around the Clock."

Finally, Allison spoke. "I went to temple with Mollie today," she said proudly. "I was the only one she invited."

"She invited me," said Frankie. "I couldn't go. I had to go somewhere with my parents."

Allison looked surprised. "She invited you?"

Frankie took a long drink of his punch. "I've

been to lots of bar mitzvahs," he said. "They have them all the time in Philly."

Allison turned to the others. "It was a bat mitzvah. Girls have bat mitzvahs, not bar mitzvahs. Mollie had to read this whole part in Hebrew and she did it all without one mistake."

"That must have been hard," said Annie.

"It wasn't so bad," said Mollie. "I've been taking Hebrew classes all year."

Travis looked at Marcus. He was studying his glass of melting yellow ice cubes. He had dressed up for the party. He wore a suit with no pocket protector and his hair was slicked down on both sides of his head making him look like Dracula in an old vampire movie. His face was Band-Aid white but considering the previous night, Travis thought he looked pretty good.

"How are you feeling today, Marcus?" asked Travis.

"Okay, as long as they're not serving pizza," said Marcus. He smiled a little. "Thanks for last night."

Cousin Seymour moved from "Edelweiss" to "Roll Out the Barrel" without missing a beat. Frankie put down his glass and turned toward the others. "Hey, why don't we go inside for a while?"

"Inside? But the party is out here," said Mollie.

"Yeah, I know," said Frankie, "but the music they're playing is for elevators."

Annie laughed and Travis glared at her. She'd never laughed at any of Frankie's jokes before. What's going on? he wondered. Was she beginning to like Frankie or something?

"Let's go inside and put on some music," said Frankie with a wink. "Maybe we can play some games of our own."

Mollie looked over at the grown-ups. "I guess no one will miss me if we go inside for a little while. But I can't stay long, I have to open my presents and thank everyone."

Frankie slipped an arm around her shoulders and pulled her toward the house. "I know this game we used to play in Philly," said Frankie. He motioned for Marcus to join them. "Come on, Turnby," he said. "We need a scorekeeper."

Annie started to follow Frankie, but Travis grabbed her arm. "You guys go on ahead. Annie and I are going to get a sandwich or something to drink," he said. Annie looked at him.

"Okay," called Frankie, "but hurry up. We can't start the game without you."

Marcus took the worn list out of his pocket. He held up three fingers, then followed the others.

The tables in the tent were filled with food. Annie and Travis loaded their paper plates with potato salad, roast beef, and crackers covered with little pink globs of something that smelled like fish. When they sat down at a long yellow table, Cousin Seymour came by to serenade them with "This Land Is Your Land." Neither one of them looked up from their food, so Cousin Seymour soon lost interest and moved on to another couple.

When they had finished, Annie pushed her plate toward the center of the table. "Do you want to go in now?" she asked.

"No," said Travis. "I don't. Any game of Murphy's is bound to be stupid. Let's stay out here and listen to the music."

"But it could be fun," insisted Annie. Travis looked up at her. There it was again. Something had changed between them. In the old days if he had said he didn't want to go in, she wouldn't have either. They would have stayed outside and made up their own games.

"I'm going in." Annie stood up and brushed the crumbs off her long blue dress. Frankie's right, he thought. She does look good in a dress. He didn't want her to go inside without him. He didn't trust Frankie.

Travis dropped his plate into one of the pink and yellow trash cans, then followed Annie into the house.

In the kitchen, a woman was arranging little sandwiches on a silver tray. "If you're looking for the other kids, they're downstairs." She pointed at the basement door.

Annie went first. The steps leading to the basement were narrow and steep. Down below, someone had pulled the blinds and only the tiniest bit of afternoon sun came through the wooden slats.

At the bottom of the steps, Travis stopped for a moment to look around. They were in a long narrow room with a Ping-Pong table, an exercise bike, and the biggest television set he'd ever seen.

"It's about time you two got here," said Frankie. The group was at the far end of the room sitting on a plaid couch. "I was just telling them that back in Philly, we used to play games at parties all the time. And we came up with this game that's a lot of fun."

He walked over to the coffee table and picked up a piece of plastic fruit. "Today we'll call it, pass the orange."

"What do you call it other days?" asked Marcus.

Frankie ignored him. "Everybody has to stand up and form a circle." He waited for a moment while they took their places. Allison crowded in beside Mollie.

"No, not that way," said Frankie. "It has to be boy, girl, boy, girl." He stepped in between Mollie and Allison. "Turnby, stand between Davis and Allison, will you?" He turned to Travis. "Are you playing or not, Marshall?"

Travis nodded and took his place between Annie and Mollie.

Frankie tossed the plastic orange in the air while he explained the game. "This is a lot like musical chairs but not as dorky," he said. "You have to pass the orange from person to person. If you drop it you're out of the game."

"That's easy enough," said Marcus. "Hand it to me."

"No dummy, you have to pass it by putting it under your chin like this." Frankie put the orange beneath his chin and held it there. "Now, without using your hands you have to give it to the other person." Frankie turned toward Allison. "Move closer," he said. "Now take this out from under my chin with your chin."

Allison stood very close. Her hands were clasped behind her back. Frankie leaned down and maneuvered the orange under her chin. "Do you have it?" he said.

"I think so," said Allison. She leaned closer trying to get a good hold on the orange.

Travis and Marcus looked at each other. Frankie had done it again. This game was a perfect way to kiss someone.

After transferring the orange, Frankie stepped back. "Good," he said. "Now, let's put some music on and turn out the the lights."

"Turn out the lights? Why should we do that?" said Mollie.

"Because it makes the game harder."

"I don't think my parents will like that," said Mollie.

"Oh, come on, Mollie," said Allison. "This is fun. I want to play this game at my party."

Frankie switched off the lamp.

"Wow, it's really dark in here," said Allison nervously. "I can barely see anyone."

"Your eyes will get used to it," said Frankie. "Now turn and pass the orange to Marcus."

Marcus leaned awkwardly toward Allison, his chin outstretched.

"You have to come closer," said Allison. "You're too far away."

Marcus moved closer. Allison tilted her head to the right to help him make the pass but Marcus let the orange slip to the floor.

"If you drop the orange, you're out of the game," Frankie said.

"No fair," said Allison, "he wasn't even trying. I shouldn't be out."

"She's right," said Marcus, "let her play." He stepped back, away from the others. "Go ahead and I'll watch."

Frankie picked up the orange and held it out to Travis. "Here, Marshall, try passing it to Davis."

Travis shook his head. "This game is stupid," he said. "Let's turn on the lights and do something else or let's go outside. I don't want to stay in here all day." He turned to Annie, waiting for her to agree, but she didn't. She looked happy.

"Don't be a party pooper, Travis," said Frankie. "This is really fun. You just have to learn how to do it." He turned to Annie. "Hey, Davis, let's me and you show them how it's done."

"No," yelled Travis, stepping in between them. "Use somebody else."

Annie patted his shoulder. "Calm down, Travis, it's only a game."

"Never mind," said Frankie. He winked at Mollie. "Come on, birthday girl, help me do this?"

Travis could see the flash of Mollie's braces as she smiled.

"Now," said Frankie, loosening his tie, "I'm going to put this orange under my chin like this." He placed it carefully under his chin for everybody to see. "Mollie, all you do is take it from me without using your hands. Okay?"

"All right," said Mollie. She stepped closer.

"Come up real close and put your chin under mine."

Mollie moved closer still, the ruffles on her yellow dress touching the lapels of Frankie's suit.

"Now tilt your head and lift your chin," he commanded.

Travis looked at Marcus. It was happening again. Any second, Frankie would make his move and there was nothing Travis could do about it.

Frankie leaned forward slowly, so that his face almost touched Mollie's. And then just as she tilted her face upward, he let the orange drop, leaned down and planted a large wet kiss right on her mouth.

No one moved. Finally Mollie stepped back and turned toward Allison, passing a silent signal between them.

Without hesitating, Allison rushed forward, pushed Mollie aside, and kissed Frankie Murphy right on the lips.

"Hey!" yelled Travis. "Don't kiss him!"

"Why not?" said Allison. "Mollie kissed him first."

"He kissed me, I didn't kiss him back," said Mollie.

"Well—" stammered Allison, "If you kiss him I want to kiss him too."

"Amazing," said Marcus. "Simply amazing." He checked two names off his list.

Frankie shrugged. "It was no big deal, it was just a birthday kiss. We did it in Philly all the time."

They heard footsteps at the top of the stairs. "Mollie, Mollie," called Mrs. Sherman, "are you down there?"

"Yes, I'm here," Mollie called out.

"What are you doing down there in the dark?" asked Mrs. Sherman. "It's time to open your presents. Come on up and bring your friends with you."

"We're coming," said Mollie. She grabbed Allison's hand and they ran up the stairs together.

Annie looked at the three boys. "I'd better go up too," she said. "Travis, are you coming?"

"In a minute," said Travis. "I have to talk to Frankie." The boys watched her march up the stairs.

Frankie reached over and switched on the light.

He picked up the plastic orange and dropped it into the wooden bowl. "What do you want to talk about?" he said.

"I think we should call the bet off," said Travis.

Frankie smiled and shook his head. "No way," he said. "A bet's a bet." He looked at Marcus for support. "Tell him, Turnby. There's only one name left. We're not stopping now, are we?"

"Yes, we are," said Travis. "Because I don't like what happened last night."

Frankie chuckled. "Me neither. When Marcus hurled his supper off the Ferris wheel, it grossed me out."

Marcus's jaw tightened. "I told Tony not to rock the chair. I told him it made me nervous."

"No," said Travis. "I don't mean that. I'm talking about the girls. When you were up there on top rocking the chair, Ricky and Katy were really scared."

Frankie shrugged. "Ah, they knew I was just kidding around. They liked it."

"But it wasn't fair the way that you kissed them." Travis fought to find the right words. "It was like . . . like . . . you tricked them."

Frankie stood up and pushed Travis aside. "Forget it, Marshall. The bet is on."

"But, it's not right," said Travis. He grabbed

Frankie's arm. "The whole thing is stupid."

Frankie whirled around. "You think it's stupid because you're losing and because your girlfriend is the only one left on the list."

Frankie pointed to Marcus. "You tell him, Turnby. It's too late to quit. Besides, this whole thing was his idea in the first place."

"Well, actually I was the one who suggested that you two should bet," said Marcus.

"Yeah, but Marshall was the one who tried to make me look bad in front of the guys, right? He's the one who said I couldn't do it."

Marcus shrugged.

Frankie walked toward the stairs. "The bet is on, Marshall, and as far as I'm concerned I've saved the best one till last."

eight

On Monday morning, Mrs. Garvy announced, "As all of you know, the sixth-grade graduation exercises will be held on Friday morning."

Marcus held up his hand. "Promotion exercises," he said. "People are promoted to seventh grade. They don't graduate."

"Thank you, Marcus," said Mrs. Garvy. "I'm so glad that you pointed that out to me." She began again. "Because the 'promotion exercises' will be held in our gym, I've been asked to appoint a decorating committee to help the custodian set up the chairs and decorate the stage. Would anyone like to volunteer?"

Everyone's hands went up. "Let me see," she said, "Annie, Frankie, why don't you two be the chairpersons of that committee?" Frankie turned around in his seat and smiled at Annie.

"And we'll have Mollie and Marcus help you."

Allison waved her hand in front of Mrs. Garvy's face. "Can I be on that committee, too, Mrs. Garvy?"

"There will be lots of committees, Allison. In fact I have your name down to be the chairperson of the refreshment committee."

"But I want to be on the same committee as Mollie," said Allison. "We're always on the same committees."

"I'm sorry, Allison," said Mrs. Garvy, "but I really need you for the refreshment table."

"Penelope?"

Penelope glanced up from her latest issue of *Wild and Free* magazine.

"I'd like you to make us each a special button to wear on that day. Make something that tells about this class and the year we've had together."

Penelope nodded happily. "I'd love to," she said. "In fact I'll start today."

"Travis, would you help Penelope with the buttons, please?"

Travis nodded, but his eyes were still on Frankie. He was waiting to see what he would try next.

Penelope studied both boys for a moment, then went back to her magazine.

Mrs. Garvy continued down her list of committee chores giving out the rest of the jobs.

Travis watched as Frankie passed Annie a note. "It's about decorating the gym," he heard Frankie whisper. "Meet me at lunchtime so we can talk about it."

As Annie read the note, she smiled. Travis felt a knot form in the pit of his stomach. She likes him, thought Travis. She actually likes that creep.

Throughout the rest of the morning Travis watched Frankie and Annie pass notes back and forth to each other. As the pile of notes on Annie's desk grew larger, so did the knot in Travis's stomach.

When lunchtime came, Annie and Frankie took their lunches to a separate table. Travis watched as, sitting off by themselves, with stacks of paper, they made drawings of the stage and lists of things needed for decorations.

Halfway through lunch Marcus joined Travis at the table. "Well, I guess she's next." He motioned toward Annie. "It's obvious that she's the only girl in the sixth-grade class Frankie hasn't kissed. So, I guess it's just a matter of time, huh?" Marcus opened his lunch bag and took out a sprouts and mushroom sandwich on rye bread.

"It isn't fair," said Travis.

"What's not fair?"

"The way he's set up all those girls," said Travis. "He pretends that he likes them and shows them all this attention, just so he can kiss them. It's not right."

Marcus took out an orange and began to peel it. "He has to do it," he said. "It's a bet."

Travis looked down at his jacket. It was really too hot to wear it now. He touched the embroidered *A* with the tip of his finger. It was frayed around the edges and he noticed the ribbed cuffs of the sleeves were dirty too.

He looked over at Annie and Frankie sitting together, their heads close as they talked. The thought of Frankie's kissing Annie made him sick, really sick. "If I'd known that it was going to end like this I never would have made that stupid bet," said Travis, stuffing his sandwich back into his lunch bag.

Marcus removed the wrapper from his straw and put it in the milk container. He took a long drink and eyed Travis carefully. "You really like Annie, don't you?" said Marcus.

"Of course, I do," said Travis. "She's been my best friend since kindergarten."

"No, I mean you *really* like her. Or you wouldn't be so upset about Frankie."

"Don't be stupid," said Travis. "It's not like Annie is my *girlfriend* or anything. It's just . . ." He looked over at her. She was laughing now, the way she always laughed with him.

"Look, Travis, it's okay if you like Annie. It's not that big a deal. We're getting older. Next year we'll all be in junior high. You and Annie, Mollie and Allison, Penelope and me, we're all growing up."

"I know that."

"Things change. Just admit it to yourself. You like Annie. You always have."

Travis hurled his paper bag into the trash basket and shoved his chair against the table. But it didn't stop him from seeing Frankie gather the sheets of papers with the plans and hand them to Annie. Frankie stood up. "Meet me after school and we can go over to the gym and measure the stage," said Frankie, so that everyone could hear. "And then after supper, I can come over to your house and shoot some baskets. I hear you have lights on your court so we can play at night." He smiled at Annie and she smiled back.

Frankie walked over to Travis. "Tonight's the night. Meet me at Davis's house after dark." He winked at Travis. "And get that jacket cleaned, will you?"

nine

The art room was a mixture of smells: turpentine, paper, oil paints, and Penelope Finchester's tomato and onion sandwich. Travis placed his clarinet case on the floor and took off his jacket and laid it over the back of a chair.

Penelope was nowhere in sight but there were signs of her everywhere. The button maker was in the middle of the table and drawings of ideas for new buttons were scattered about.

Travis checked his watch. He had a Boy Scout meeting at seven and he still had to get home and change. They'd have to work hard if they were to get fifteen buttons completed by tomorrow.

Penelope and Marcus came out of the art closet loaded down with construction paper, Magic Markers, and stacks of newsprint. The two of them were laughing and talking like old friends. They stopped when they saw Travis.

"Gee," said Marcus, "we didn't hear you come in."

"It's hard to hear inside a closet," said Travis. "What were you two doing in there?"

Marcus and Penelope looked at each other and then back at Travis.

Finally, Penelope said, "Marcus brought by some designs for my bird refuge."

"That's right," said Marcus. "Penelope has this crazy idea about building a bird refuge in the city park this summer and I'm going to help her."

"Since when do you care so much about birds?" said Travis.

Marcus looked at Penelope and smiled. "Since I learned that birds migrate to the same destination every year. It raises some interesting scientific questions, don't you think?"

Penelope beamed at him.

"Besides," said Marcus, "some birds are pretty nice once you get to know them." He smiled at Penelope. "Especially odd birds, they're the best."

Penelope smiled back at Marcus. "Yes," she said

softly, "odd birds should really stick together when they find one another."

Travis couldn't tell what the two of them were talking about, but he was pretty sure it wasn't just about birds.

Marcus dropped the art supplies on the table. "I've got to go," he said. "I have a math meet over at the high school." He picked up his books and headed toward the door. "I'll call you later."

Marcus was out the door and down the hall before Travis realized that Marcus hadn't been talking to him.

Penelope arranged the supplies on the table. On her sweatshirt was one of her own creations, a button which said BIKES NOT BOMBS.

"What's that?" asked Travis.

Penelope touched the bright red badge. "This? Oh, it's for a group that sends bicycles to South America. Down there, people use bikes for transportation because they're too poor to buy cars."

"How do you know about all these things?" asked Travis.

"I read a lot. How about you?"

"Read? Sure, sometimes, but usually I'm too busy with music and scouting and stuff like that."

Penelope nodded as if she understood. She picked up an art pencil and pointed to one of the sketches. "I've been working on some ideas for tomorrow's ceremonies. I thought we could use this green paper for the background." She pushed a stack of construction paper toward Travis. "It's the end of the year and that's all we have left."

Travis picked up a picture of a sixth-grader with a graduation cap. "Is this what you're thinking of using?"

Penelope shrugged. "Maybe. I was waiting to see what ideas you have."

"I'm not much of an artist," said Travis. "But I drew up some ideas in English class that I thought that we could use." He leaned back in his chair. "Mrs. Garvy wants the button to show something about this year. Something that tells about us as a group."

Penelope nibbled on the end of her pencil for a moment. Her eyes were clear and bright now, like one of those fragile dolls you see in the windows of antiques stores.

Travis watched as she drew a sketch of a basketball hoop. Each stroke of the pen was smooth and clean. She was a good artist.

"Annie and our team won the city basketball league championship," said Penelope. "We could put a big basketball in the center of the button with a six on it."

Travis shook his head. "But that doesn't include the boys," he said. "Hey, I have an idea. Remember, back in March when we cleaned up the ground all around school and planted three trees?"

"I remember," said Penelope. "I made you buttons to wear that said MOTHER EARTH DAY, MARCH 12, CLEAN UP YOUR ROOM!"

"That's right." Travis remembered how he had to beg the other Boy Scouts to wear Penelope's buttons. "We even painted the swing set for the kindergarten playground. Let's make a button for that."

Penelope shook her head. "We can't. You organized it through the Boy Scouts, the girls didn't do anything."

"But you made the buttons."

"Nope," said Penelope. "We have to come up with something that involved both the boys and girls in the sixth grade." She tapped the eraser on her teeth.

"Well, I have something that might work," said Travis. He picked up a pencil and began to make a few lines. "It's like the one I started in English class. Reach in my jacket pocket and get that piece of paper for me."

Penelope stood up and walked over to the jacket.

"I drew this picture of two schools, one is the elementary, the other is the junior high. We could put a kid walking between them showing that he's moving up."

Travis glanced up from the sketch he was making to see Penelope holding the kiss list. "Wait a minute," he yelled, "that's not it." He grabbed for the list but Penelope pulled it away.

"What is this?" she asked. "Why do all these girls' names have checks beside them?"

Travis's mind rushed through all the reasons he would have a list of sixth-grade girls. "It's for the buttons," he said. "I was trying to count how many we had to make."

"I don't think so," she said. "You only have the girls' names here, no boys. And everybody's name has a check beside it but Annie's." Penelope dangled the list out of his reach. "Travis, tell me the truth. What is this list for?"

Travis slumped down in his chair. He wanted to tell her, he wanted to explain, but he couldn't. "I can't tell you," he said.

"This has something to do with Frankie, right?"

Travis shook his head. "Penelope, I can't tell you, just give me back the list. Okay?"

"My name is on top," she said. "I know this has something to do with me and Frankie Murphy and the rest of the girls. What is it?"

"The whole thing is stupid. Just forget it."

She leaned forward, "Everybody's name but Annie's is checked off. Why not Annie?" Penelope touched his sleeve. "Look, I know you're upset," she said. "I saw the way Frankie was flirting with Annie today, but it doesn't mean anything. He does that with all the girls. Remember how he acted with me?" She looked at the list again. "Wait a minute," she said, "now I get it. This list is in order of all the girls that Frankie has liked this year. But why are these checks here?"

Travis stood up.

"Is this a list of every girl he's gone with? Every girl he's kissed?"

Travis jerked the list from her hands. "I can't tell you. I promised all the guys," he said. "I can't tell you."

Penelope studied him for a long time. When she spoke her voice had a cool hard edge to it. "Never mind, Travis, you don't have to tell me," she said. "I think I get the picture now."

"Penelope, I've got to go. I have a scout meeting and I have to get home and change clothes. Maybe I can come over to your house after the meeting and we can do these buttons."

Penelope shook her head. "Don't bother," she

said. "I can take care of this without you." She gathered up the paper and pencils scattered around the table.

"Penelope, don't be mad," said Travis.

Penelope threw the button maker and the green paper into her book bag. "Why shouldn't I be mad?" she said. "I thought you liked me."

"I do like you."

"Then how could you have gone along with this list of Frankie's? How could you have stood by and let him make a fool of me?"

"He didn't make a fool of you," insisted Travis. "That night at the roller rink, people thought Frankie was the jerk, not you."

She cinched up the book bag and threw it over her shoulder. "I'm right then. It is a kiss list. And for some reason you were part of it." She picked up the drawings of the bird refuge Marcus had made her. "What about Marcus and the rest of the boys? Are they part of this thing too?"

"Yes, I mean no, not exactly. It's too complicated to explain."

Penelope slipped the drawings under her arm and walked toward the door. "Go on to your scout meeting, Travis. I'll take care of the buttons."

"But we didn't come up with an idea yet."

Penelope turned and glared at him. "I'll do it myself. I don't want your help." With that she walked out of the art room and slammed the door behind her. Travis crammed the list into his pocket and grabbed his clarinet case and the jacket off the chair, but by the time he got to the hallway she was gone.

ten

From the gate Travis could see Reed teetering on the back of the front porch swing. His Superman cape dangled from his shoulders as he tried to balance.

"Reed," screamed Travis. "Are you crazy? Get down from there before you fall."

"Don't bother me," Reed yelled. "I'm trying to fly." He gripped the heavy chain that attached the swing to the porch ceiling. "I just have to get my balance here."

Travis raced toward the porch taking the steps in one jump.

As Reed let go of the chain, hands out in perfect

flying position, the swing jerked backward. Reed tumbled forward over the top of the swing. Travis reached out and caught him in midair. "See?" yelled Travis. "What did I tell you? You can't fly from there."

Reed struggled against Travis.

"Yes, I can. I just need to get up higher so my cape works."

Travis lowered Reed to the ground. His heart was pounding loud and fast. "If I hadn't come along just now you would have fallen and broken your head," yelled Travis. "You shouldn't climb up on a swing like that, it's dangerous! From now on, stay off that thing."

Reed wriggled out of Travis's grip. "You're not my boss," said Reed, "Annie is." He pulled his cape tighter around his shoulders. "I don't have to listen to what you say." Pushing Travis aside, he walked over to the steps and sat down.

"Look, Reed, I'm telling you for your own good. Don't go climbing up on things like that. It's okay to run around and pretend but sooner or later you've got to learn. You're not Superman and you can't fly."

Reed put his fingers in his ears.

Travis sat down beside him and slipped his arm

around Reed's shoulders. "Look, buddy," said Travis, "I'm just trying to tell you this for your own good. You gave me a scare just now." Reed pulled away.

"Hey, what do you say if I come over tomorrow and give you your first clarinet lesson?"

"Clarinet playing is for sissies," said Reed.

"Sissies, uh?" Travis stood up and walked down the steps. "Where's Annie?"

"She's out back," mumbled Reed, "playing basketball with Frankie Murphy."

Travis nodded and continued walking.

"Frankie Murphy is nicer than you," yelled Reed. "He doesn't boss me around. I like him better and so does Annie."

When he got to the back, Travis saw Frankie and Annie playing one on one under the lights. Travis halted and stayed in the shadows, watching and listening.

White tennis shoes gleamed as Annie and Frankie circled each other under the hoop. The ball seemed to twirl on their fingertips as it passed between them.

When Frankie drove forward down the court to make the shot, Annie was there, guarding the move. When he edged to the left, her hands went up. When he dodged to the right, she blocked his shot. They moved around the court like two dancers; every action was smooth and graceful.

As they played they talked like old friends. "So, you were trying to explain how you got here," said Annie.

"Usual way." Frankie smiled. "I had two parents."

"No, silly, I mean to Harpersville."

Frankie intercepted the ball and began bouncing it with an easy slow rhythm just out of Annie's reach. "My father was transferred here," continued Frankie. "Mom and I didn't want to come. We didn't want to leave everybody we knew back in Philly." He bounced the ball harder. "I told Dad it was going to be awful but he wouldn't listen."

"What's so bad about it?"

"Oh, nothing, just that everybody's been together since they were in strollers." He stopped and looked at Annie. "It's hard to break in."

"What are you talking about?" said Annie.

"I'm talking about you and Travis and Marcus and Mollie and the rest of the kids. You guys have known one another since you were little." He pounded the ball into the cement with his hand. "It's not that easy to come into a new town in the middle of sixth grade, you know. People aren't that nice."

"We tried to be. You were always putting us down," said Annie. "And it makes people mad the way you always compare Harpersville to Philly."

Frankie shrugged. "What's to compare? This whole town looks like it was taken off the front of some corny greeting card. I hate it." He tossed the ball at her. "Come on, are we playing ball or not?"

She scooped up the ball and threw it up and over his head. "That's two," she said.

"Hey," Frankie laughed. "I wasn't ready." With an easy jump, he caught the rebound and dribbled the ball down the court. Annie was smiling. She seemed to like the challenge of playing against someone her equal.

Frankie faked left then went right and put the ball up and into the basket.

"Good one," yelled Annie.

Travis kept watching from the shadows as the game proceeded.

Every so often he would hear Annie say "nice shot," as Frankie threw one up and over her head.

They're both tall and good-looking, thought Travis, both athletes, both popular. They were perfectly matched as if they belonged together.

Wait! Did Frankie really like Annie or was he just being nice so that he could kiss her? Travis had to find out. He stepped out of the shadows and onto the court.

"Hi, Travis," Annie said.

Frankie took his shot and missed. He caught the ball with his right hand and tucked it under his arm.

"I thought you had a Boy Scout meeting tonight," said Annie.

Frankie pointed to Travis's Boy Scout uniform. "Nice outfit, Marshall. Do you always dress like that or just when you're out doing good deeds?"

"Everybody wears a uniform to the meeting," said Travis.

"Travis, do you want to shoot some baskets with us?"

"He's not here to play basketball," said Frankie. "He came over because we have a little business to do tonight."

"What kind of business?"

"Boy stuff," said Frankie. He motioned toward the house. "Have anything in there to drink? I'm really thirsty."

"I get the feeling you're trying to get rid of me," Annie said.

"No, of course not," said Frankie. "Me and Travis

just got something to settle. We need time to talk."

Annie bit the bottom of her lip. Travis knew that look. She was mad, but he couldn't decide who she was angry with—him or Frankie.

"Is my little brother still out front?" she asked.

"I saw him out there when I came in."

"I'd better go check on him," she said. "He's awfully quiet." Annie walked toward the front of the house. "I'll be right back. In the meantime, you two can go ahead with your boy stuff. I wouldn't want to interfere."

Travis watched her walk away, back straight, hands clenched. No doubt about it, he thought, she's mad.

"Nice girl," said Frankie. "And not a bad basketball player either."

"Not bad?" protested Travis. "She had you going out there."

Frankie laughed. "Are you kidding? I wasn't even trying. I was just playing around till you got here," he said. "I see you're wearing my jacket." Frankie reached out and brushed some imaginary dust off Travis's shoulder.

The jacket, thought Travis. This is all happening because of this stupid jacket of mine. Why didn't he see it before? The bet, the kissing, the list, all because Frankie wanted his jacket. It wasn't worth it.

Travis tore off his jacket and threw it at Frankie. "Here," he said. "Take it and get out! You win."

"What are you doing?" said Frankie. "I haven't even kissed her yet."

"You don't have to. The jacket's yours. Just get out of here and leave Annie and me alone."

Frankie held the jacket for a moment and looked at it. "I don't get it. You and Marcus said I had to kiss every girl on the list. That was the bet."

"Well—" stammered Travis, "I'm changing things. Six girls is enough. You proved your point. But I don't want any part of it. The whole thing is stupid and mean."

"What are you talking about?"

"I mean that kissing girls when you don't really like them isn't right. You shouldn't treat girls like that."

"But girls like to be kissed."

"Maybe they do, but not the way you're doing it." Travis checked to see if Annie was coming. "Look, Frankie, you win," he whispered. "The jacket's yours. Now get out of here before she comes back."

Frankie threw the jacket over his shoulder and

tossed the ball to Travis. "Thanks, Marshall. It was nice doing business with you." He walked away, then stopped and turned around. "Wait a minute," said Frankie, "Now, I get it. You like her, don't you? You want me out of here because you don't want me to kiss her."

"Leave, Murphy."

"No way," said Frankie. "I'm staying. Just to show you I can do it."

"I told you you don't have to. You win. Now get out of here."

Frankie smiled and put on the jacket. "But I don't like leaving a job till it's finished. I'm a man of my word."

The back door opened and Annie came out carrying four cans of soda. The door swung shut behind her with a loud click.

"Oh, darn it," said Annie. "I think maybe I locked us out." She looked worried. "Mom is working late tonight. And we never found Reed's key. What will we do?"

"It's okay. We can stay out here till your mom comes home," said Frankie. "We've got the soda, the basketball, what more could we want?"

Annie set the sodas down on the picnic table. "I feel so stupid locking us out like that."

Frankie strolled over and picked up a can of soda. "You know, Annie, I was just telling Marshall here the same thing. I like to do things perfectly too." He handed a soda to Annie. "For instance, take scores. You like perfect scores, don't you?"

"What are you talking about? And why do you have on Travis's jacket?"

"He gave it to me. Didn't you, Marshall?"

"Annie, can we talk?" said Travis. "There's something I have to tell you."

"Travis wouldn't give you his *A*'s jacket. He loves that thing."

"Right," said Frankie. "But there's something he loves more . . . much more." Frankie snickered. "You see, me and your good friend Travis here had this little bet that involves you."

"Frankie," said Travis. "Don't. Let me tell her."

Frankie threw up his hands. "All right, then you tell her. Tell your girlfriend how I got this jacket from you."

"What's he talking about?"

Travis stared at Annie as he tried to find the words to explain to her. She would hate Frankie for the list, but she'd hate him even more for going along with it.

"Hey, what's this?" Frankie pulled a tattered

piece of paper from the pocket of Travis's jacket. Unfolding it carefully, he held it up to the light. "Hey, what do you know? Marcus made you one too." He shoved the paper into Annie's face. "Take a look. This is a list of all the girls in the sixth grade."

Annie read the list. "Why is there a check by everybody's name but mine?"

"Come on, Marshall," said Frankie. "Either you tell her or I will."

Travis opened his mouth but before he could say anything, he heard a scream. It was Reed.

Annie turned and raced toward the front of the house. The boys ran after her.

Out front, on the ground, lay Reed, his face covered with blood. He was crying and holding his right arm against his chest.

"What happened?" asked Annie.

"I was trying to fly and I fell," cried Reed. "Annie, my arm really hurts."

"Quick," said Travis, "call 911."

Annie ran to the front door and turned the knob. "I can't," she said. "The doors are locked."

"My arm hurts," cried Reed, again. The blood flowed from a cut on his lower lip.

"We need something to stop the bleeding," yelled Travis. "Quick, Frankie, there's a handkerchief in my jacket. Give it to me!"

Frankie's face was white.

"Frankie, did you hear me? I need the handkerchief from my pocket. Hand it to me."

Frankie gave him the handkerchief and looked away. "I don't like blood," he told them. "It makes me sick."

Travis pressed the handkerchief tightly against Reed's lip to stop the bleeding. "The cut isn't as bad as it looks," said Travis. He touched Reed's arm gently. "Can you wiggle your fingers?"

"I think so," said Reed. He moved all five to prove the point.

"You're going to be okay," said Travis. "It's not broken. Sprained maybe, but you'll be all right."

"How do you know?" sobbed Reed.

Travis pointed to his Boy Scout sash. "First aid, remember? I spent a whole afternoon over here putting bandages on you and Annie. I'm an expert."

Reed smiled a little, his lip swollen and bloody.

"Blood makes me sick," said Frankie, again. "I don't want any part of it."

"Stay here," said Annie. "I'll go next door to the Martins'."

"NO!" screamed Reed. "Don't leave me."

Annie looked at Travis. "What are we going to do?" she said. Her voice sounded high and shaky.

"Travis," whispered Reed. "I don't feel so good."

Travis pushed the hair back from Reed's sweaty face. "Maybe we better have somebody look at him," said Travis. "His arm is swelling up. And he's going into shock."

"Why don't we carry him over to the Martins'?" said Annie. "They'll know what to do."

"How can we carry him?"

"By linking arms," said Annie. "We do it all the time in basketball."

"Good idea," said Travis. "Reed, we're going to lift you up and take you next door to the Martins'. Now, just hold on. Everything is going to be fine."

Travis and Annie carefully lifted Reed up between them and started toward the gate.

"Frankie, go over to the Martins' and tell them that we're coming," said Travis.

No answer.

Annie and Travis looked around. Frankie was gone. Travis's jacket lay on the ground.

eleven

"I'm cold," Reed said. "And my arm hurts."

"Quick," said Travis. "Put my jacket around him."

"But your jacket will get all bloody," said Annie.

"It doesn't matter. He's cold because he's in shock. We have to keep him warm." Travis helped Annie drape the jacket around Reed's shoulders and zipped it closed.

"If the Martins aren't home, what are we going to do?" She slid her arms under Reed and locked hands with Travis again. Reed was heavier than he looked.

"We can carry him down to my house and call

911 from there," said Travis. He tried to keep his voice calm.

Half walking, half running, the two of them carried Reed toward the sidewalk. As they opened the front gate, the lights of Mrs. Davis's station wagon appeared. She stopped the car and jumped out.

"What's going on? What happened to Reed?"

"Reed was trying to fly," Annie said. "He cut his lip and he really hurt his arm."

Mrs. Davis reached out and gently touched Reed's arm. "We should have a doctor look at this."

"We were going to call 911 for help," said Travis, "but the door blew shut and we were locked out."

"It's all my fault, Mom," said Annie. "I should have taken better care of him."

"Maybe so," said Mrs. Davis, "but Reed knows he can't fly. Don't you, Reed?"

Reed nodded. His face was still wet from tears, but his crying had slowed to an occasional hiccup.

Mrs. Davis took a shiny new key from her pocket and handed it to Annie. "You two go on inside and wait for me. I'm going to drive Reed to the emergency room. They'll have to X-ray his arm."

"But I don't want an X ray," said Reed. "X rays hurt."

"No, they don't," said Travis. "Superman does it

all the time. Haven't you heard of X-ray vision?"

"That's when Superman stares right through people."

"The doctors at the hospital do the same thing only they use a machine."

Reed looked down at his swollen arm. "I'll go as long as it doesn't hurt."

"Travis," said Mrs. Davis, "could you wait with Annie till I get back?"

"Sure," said Travis, "I'd be glad to."

"Can I still wear your jacket to the hospital?" asked Reed.

"Okay, but no flying in it." Travis opened the car door for Mrs. Davis.

After her mother drove away, Annie turned to Travis. "You were great, tonight. The way that you stopped the bleeding and covered him up. You knew just what to do."

"Yeah, but you were the one who figured out how to carry him. I'd never have thought of that."

Annie gave him a gentle shove. "I guess together we're a pretty good team."

Travis took a deep breath. "Now that all the excitement is over, Annie, we've got to talk."

She reached into her pocket and pulled out the list. "About this?"

Travis took the list from her and read it out loud. "Penelope, Terry, Katy, Ricky, Mollie, and Allison. These are all people I have to talk to tomorrow."

"Why?"

"Over the past few weeks, I've been really stupid, Annie. I owe you and all these other girls an apology."

"This has something to do with why Frankie had your jacket, doesn't it?"

"But it isn't just Frankie," said Travis. "It was me and Marcus—it was all of us."

Travis sat down on the swing and Annie joined him. "Earlier tonight, I was standing in the dark watching you two play ball," said Travis. "I heard him tell you about how hard it was to come here in the middle of the year and try to be part of the group."

"Was he just making that up?"

"No, I think he was telling the truth," said Travis. "I think he brags all the time because he wants to belong."

"But that doesn't explain why he goes around putting everybody down."

"He's just trying to impress us. People do a lot of stupid things when they're trying to be cool."

"Maybe," said Annie, "but what does that have to do with this list?"

"The list is my fault," said Travis. "I was so fed up with his bragging that I made a bet with him."

"What kind of bet?"

"I bet him that he couldn't kiss all the girls in the class before the end of the school year."

"Are you crazy? Why would you do something like that?"

"I know, I know. It was really stupid. But at the time I didn't know that it would hurt anybody."

"And did it?"

"It hurt a lot of people and I'm sorry. I should have stopped it but I was afraid of what the guys would say."

"Why are you telling me this now?"

"Because today when I saw you with Frankie I realized that Marcus and Penelope were right. Birds have to stick together and so do friends."

Annie shook her head. "I don't understand, Travis. And I don't like the thought of you betting on something as important as kissing."

Travis took the key from Annie's hand. "Let's go inside and sit down," he said. "I'll tell you everything right from the beginning. And I'll try to explain how this whole thing got out of hand."

She pointed to the list. "And will you tell me why my name is the very last and why there's no check beside it?"

"That's easy," said Travis. He tore her name off the bottom of the paper. "This big list belongs to Frankie Murphy with a check by all the girls he's kissed this year. And this list—" he held up Annie's name—"is mine."

"Will my name get a check too?" she asked.

"Maybe," said Travis, "when the time is right. But if there is a check it will be because we both want to and not because of some stupid bet."

Travis stood up and unlocked the door. He held it open for Annie.

"It makes me mad to think that Frankie got away with this," said Annie. "He's been mean to so many girls. It just isn't fair."

"I'm sorry, Annie."

Annie bit her lip. "And Penelope, that night at the roller rink, how he just kissed her and then skated away with somebody else. She didn't deserve that."

"Penelope knows about Frankie," said Travis. "She found the list in my pocket." Travis followed Annie into the house and closed the door. "I've been a real jerk about this and I wish I could do something to make it up to you."

"There's nothing you can do about Frankie now," said Annie. "Tomorrow is the last day of school."

"Maybe there is," said Travis. "Let's talk about it." They talked for a long time.

It was after nine when Mrs. Davis and Reed came home. Reed was wearing a bandage around his arm.

"You were right, Travis," said Mrs. Davis, "Reed's arm was only sprained. But there will be no more flying for at least six weeks. Bed, right?"

Reed nodded. "Travis, can you come over tomorrow and teach me something on the clarinet?"

"You won't be able to play with that arm of yours," said Travis. "But if you want I could come over and give a private little concert for you."

"Do you know any songs from *Sesame Street*?"

"Of course," said Travis. "Your sister and I grew up with Big Bird and Oscar."

Annie smiled at Travis as she gave Reed a hug. "You better go on to bed," she said.

Mrs. Davis carried Reed upstairs.

"I have to go now," said Travis. "There's some calls I want to make tonight."

"Will you pick me up for school tomorrow?"

"You bet," said Travis. "I have an idea that tomorrow is going to be a big day for all of us."

twelve

The next morning Travis was at Annie's house early. It was the last day they would ever walk to King Elementary School together, he thought. The last day they would spend in sixth grade, the last time the class would be together before junior high.

Annie came to the door. She was wearing the blue dress she'd worn to Mollie's party and was carrying Travis's jacket. "My Mom washed it for you last night. There's a couple of stains on it from Reed's bloody lip that she couldn't get out. I'm sorry."

"Would you like to wear it?" he asked.

Annie looked at him. "But this is your favorite jacket, Travis. You always wear it."

"I know, that's why I'd like you to wear it today." He paused trying to think of how he could put the next part. "I want you to wear it to show everybody that . . . we're friends . . . good friends."

Annie smiled at him and put the jacket on. "Come on," she said. "We don't want to be late on our last day of school."

They walked together toward school. "After I left last night, I called Penelope," said Travis. "I wanted to apologize about the bet I made with Frankie and explain how everything happened."

"What did she say?"

"She'd already figured out what the list meant, but I think she was mad at me for going along with it."

"I was too," said Annie.

"That's why I decided I had to make it up to the two of you. You were right last night when you said it wasn't fair that Frankie got away with all this."

"What are you going to do?" Annie looked toward the school. "You aren't going to fight him or anything stupid like that, are you?"

"Of course not," said Travis. "Fighting Frankie wouldn't solve anything. You have to hit him where it hurts."

"How do we do that?"

"Last night I had an idea of how all the girls can get even with Frankie. And when I told Penelope she said she'd help me."

"What are you going to do?"

Travis took Annie's hand in his. "Just wait and see. You're going to like it."

The school yard was filled with the families of all the sixth graders.

Next to the door of the gym, where the ceremony was to be, stood Frankie, Tony, Marcus, and the rest of the boys.

Travis waved but stayed with Annie. He didn't want to talk to Frankie or the others right now.

On the other side of the playground, Penelope was surrounded by the sixth-grade girls. She had on a long yellow dress and big butterfly earrings that bobbed in the morning breeze. She was passing buttons out to the girls. Every time a girl read the message she began to laugh.

"Hey, Annie," yelled Mollie, "come get your button. We made one for each of us. You'll love it!"

"What's going on?" asked Annie.

Travis grinned. "Last night after I talked to Penelope, I called Mollie and Allison. When I told them about the list, they were really mad. But after I apologized and they calmed down, they said they would help. The four of us were up till after midnight working on my plan."

"What plan?" asked Annie.

"Do you remember how Mrs. Garvy asked Penelope and me to make buttons for today?" said Travis.

"Yes," said Annie. "You had to come up with a pin design of something that happened during the year."

"She also said it had to do with what involved both the boys and girls. Well I think we've done that. Just watch."

The morning bell rang. Penelope picked up another bag from the ground and winked at the girls. "Ladies, are we ready?" she asked.

"Absolutely," Mollie replied. "Let's go!"

Penelope pulled out a whistle from the bag and blew. The girls lined up behind her. Two more short blasts and Penelope and the girls marched across the playground toward Frankie Murphy and the boys.

"Mr. Murphy," yelled Penelope, "front and center."

The adults stopped talking and stared at Penelope and the girls. "Are they holding the promotion exercises out here?" someone asked. "Last year they had the whole thing inside."

Penelope turned to the crowd. "Ladies and gentlemen, this isn't part of the regular promotion exercises. But we wanted to have a special ceremony for all the male members of our class."

Penelope turned back to the boys. "We know all about the list," she said. "And we know about the bet. We've talked it over and we're really mad."

"Go on, Penelope, you tell them," said Allison.

"For the past seven years we've been friends, good friends. And next year when we go to junior high we're going to need one another more than ever." She looked over at Marcus. "Friends have got to stick together."

Marcus was concentrating on the tips of his shiny black shoes.

"We're willing to forgive you if you'll wear these." Penelope reached in and took out a bright green button. It said I'VE BEEN A SIXTH-GRADE JERK.

"No way," said Frankie. "I'm not going to wear that. Are you crazy?"

Travis stepped forward. "Throw one over here, Penelope. I'll put it on."

Mollie took a pin from Penelope's bag and hurled it at him.

"Give me one too," said Marcus. "It sums up precisely how we all acted, Penelope."

"Oh, all right," said Tony Foley. "I'll wear one. I don't want every girl I know to be mad at me for the rest of junior high."

Allison smiled and pinned a green "jerk" button on Tony's suit jacket. One by one the other boys shuffled forward and reluctantly took buttons and put them on. Every boy but Frankie.

"Hey, wait a minute," said Marcus. "What are you girls going to wear?"

"We were hoping you'd ask," said Mollie. "Last night Penelope, Allison, and I made some special pins for all of the girls." She smiled at Penelope. "Just say the word," she whispered, "we're ready."

"Ladies," said Penelope in a loud clear voice, "attach your pins!"

The girls reached into their pockets and took out bright green buttons and pinned them over their hearts.

The boys leaned forward so they could read the words.

"Wait a minute," yelled Frankie. "You can't wear those buttons in there." He motioned to the gym. "It's not fair."

Penelope arched an eyebrow, "Fair," she said. "Was your list fair to us?"

"But it was just a joke," Frankie said. "I didn't

mean anything by it." He turned to the other boys. "Do you believe this?" he asked. "These girls can't even take a joke. In Philly girls used to laugh at stuff like this."

"Well, you're not in Philly, now," said Penelope. "Come on, girls, we don't want to be late." With one long whistle blast in Frankie's ear, she shoved him aside and marched toward the gym door. The girls followed.

"I don't get it. What do those buttons say?" said Annie.

Travis reached into the pocket of his suit jacket. "Here," said Travis. "I made one especially for you. Even though you don't know this from experience, I thought you would want to wear it."

Annie took the pin from his hand and looked at it. She began to laugh. "You bet I want to wear this. It's perfect." She fastened the pin onto the jacket. "I'm ready, if you are," said Annie. "Let's go in."

As they passed by Frankie Murphy, Annie smiled and pointed to her pin. The same pin every other sixth-grade girl was wearing.

FRANKIE MURPHY IS THE WORLD'S WORST KISSER!

ABOUT THE AUTHOR

Donna Guthrie was born in Washington, Pennsylvania, and was graduated from Rider College in New Jersey. A former teacher, she is the author of several books for young readers, including *The Witch Who Lives down the Hall*, *The Witch Has an Itch*, and *Mrs. Gigglebelly Is Coming for Tea*.

Donna Guthrie lives in Los Gatos, California, with her husband and two children.

AD	FF	JUL 0 1 94	MU
AV	GR		NC
BO	HI		SJ
CL	HO		CN L
DS	LS		